THE HAUNTING OF WAINRICH MANOR

A MYSTERY SEARCHERS BOOK

BARRY FORBES

THE HAUNTING OF WAINRICH MANOR

A MYSTERY SEARCHERS BOOK

VOLUME 10

By
BARRY FORBES

BAKKEN
BOOKS

ISBN 978-1-955657-27-3
For Worldwide Distribution
Printed in the U.S.A.

Published by Bakken Books
2022

PRAISE FOR BARRY FORBES AND THE MYSTERY SEARCHERS FAMILY BOOK SERIES

AMAZING BOOK! My daughter is in 6th grade and she is homeschooled, she really enjoyed reading this book. Highly recommend to middle schoolers. *Rubi Pizarro on Amazon*

I have three boys 11-15 and finding a book they all like is sometimes a challenge This series is great! My 15-year-old said, "I actually like it better than Hardy Boys because it tells me currents laws about technology that I didn't know." My reluctant 13-year-old picked it up without any prodding and that's not an easy feat. *Shantelshomeschool on Instagram*

I stumbled across the author and his series on Instagram and had to order the first book! Fun characters, good storyline too, easy reading. Best for ages 11 and up. *AZmommy2011 on Amazon*

Virtues of kindness, leadership, compassion, responsibility, loyalty, courage, diligence, perseverance, loyalty and service are characterized throughout the book. *Lynn G. on Amazon*

Barry, he LOVED it! My son is almost 14 and enjoys reading but most books are historical fiction or non-fiction. He carried your book everywhere, reading in any spare moments. He can't wait for book 2 – I'm ordering today and book 3 for his birthday. *Ourlifeathome on Instagram*

Perfect series for our 7th grader! I'm thrilled to have come across this perfect series for my 13-year old son this summer. We purchased the entire set! They are easy, but captivating reads and he is enjoying them very much. *Amylcarney on Amazon*

Great "clean" page turner! My son was hooked after the first three chapters and kept asking me to read more... Fast forward three hours and we were done! When you read a book in one sitting, you know it is a good one. *Homework and Horseplay on Amazon*

"Great book for kids and no worry for parents! I bought and read this book with my grandson in mind. What a great book! The plot was well done using the sleuths' knowledge of modern technology to solve this mystery." *Regina Krause on Amazon*

"Take a break, wander away from the real world into the adventurous life of spunky kids out to save the world in the hidden hills of the Southwest." *Ron Boat on Amazon*

"Books so engaging my teenager woke up early and stayed up late to finish the story. After the first book, he asked: Are there more in this series? We HAVE to get them! He even chipped in some cash to buy more books." *Sabrinakaadventures on Instagram*

DISCLAIMER

Prescott, the former capital of the Arizona Territory, is considered by many to be the state's crown jewel. Aside from this Central Arizona locale, The Mystery Searchers Family Book Series is a work of fiction. Names, characters, businesses, places, events, incidents, and other locales are either the products of the author's imagination or used in a fictitious manner. Any resemblance to actual persons, living or dead, or actual events is purely coincidental.

Read more at www.MysterySearchers.com.

For Linda,
whose steadfast love and encouragement
made this series possible

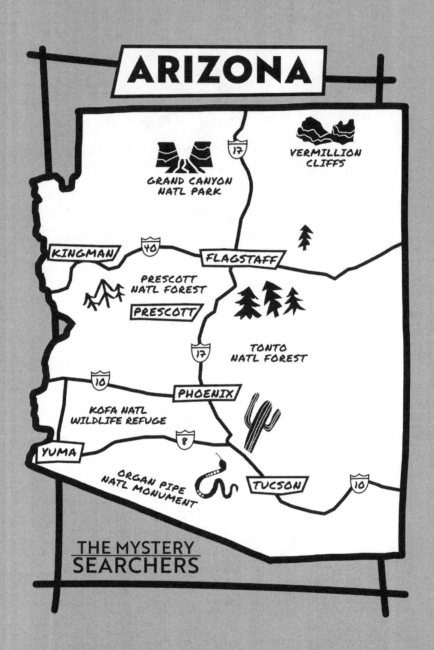

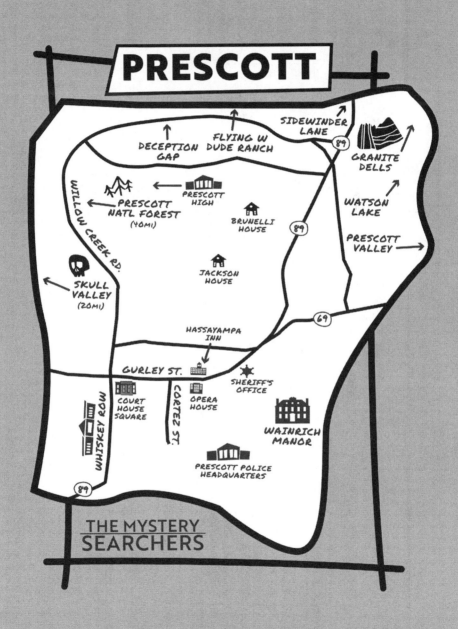

1

THE TARGET

"This place is downright spooky," Kathy said, her voice hushed.

Pete squinted in the dark, cold night. "Well, duh. Anytime there are ghosts running around . . ."

Kathy clucked like a hen. "You and your ghosts."

Pete grinned. He loved annoying his sister.

It was close to midnight. For the past hour, the lookalike siblings had scrunched down, sheltering behind a line of barren oak trees, their eyes locked on the forsaken One Wainrich Manor. Their hiding place afforded views of the front of the imposing three-story mansion, which faced east, and the side of the house, facing south. *Dark as the ace of spades.*

They had been in the same position for so long that Kathy had developed leg cramps. *Not to mention being half frozen,* she brooded. Moonlight reflected off patches of white, the remnants of a recent after-Christmas snowfall in Prescott. A million stars winked down at them. Lying on the hard, cold ground—with nothing between them and the earth but a thin, old comforter—was a sure recipe for torture. Plus, she hated stakeouts with a passion. Above all, there was the boredom factor. Time crawled by in slow motion.

As the minutes clicked toward midnight, Pete began losing hope. Kathy checked her cellphone for the umpteenth time. "We're outta here in fifteen," she insisted. "Not another—"

"*There it is!*" Pete blurted. A flickering light had materialized on the manor's darkened third floor, glimmering through a dormer window. *Well, well.* The phenomenon had appeared just as Mrs. Robertson—Roberta, as she had insisted the siblings call her—had claimed it would. Next, she had said, it would work its way into the basement. *Why?* At this stage, there were no answers. Only questions.

Down, down went the quivering glow, reappearing in the windows of the second floor just moments later as it continued its journey through the mansion. Not that they could see its movement on the staircase—no windows there. The light vanished again. If it followed the path Roberta had first witnessed, then it would skip the ground floor and, well . . .

The mystery searchers had scouted the manor more than once. They knew the basement was windowless. Still, there was a multi-sided glass hatch on the south side of the home that topped what used to be a coal chute, a relic from the century before. Yellowed with age, filthy with grime, the multiple panes of glass hid whatever rested—or moved—beneath.

The siblings waited with bated breath, but not for long.

There. From inside the hatch, the glow filtered through the grimy glass. *Right where Roberta had said it would.* It seemed to float in the air forever. The two watched, transfixed, when—to their astonishment—the hatch opened upward with, seemingly, nothing beneath to push it open except the strange light. A few moments passed before the cover lowered and the quivering glow vanished. Darkness returned to One Wainrich Manor.

"Creepy!" Kathy whispered, grabbing her brother's arm

without realizing it. Adrenalin coursed through her body. Her face was flushed, and she no longer felt frozen. Although Kathy emphatically did not believe in ghosts, she had a visceral reaction to uncanny phenomena.

Pete remained calm. "Did it—whatever *it* is—just escape from that open hatch?" he wondered aloud.

"There's no 'it,' there *can't* be an 'it,'" his sister chided. "Nothing escaped and whoever's still inside must be human."

"How do you know?"

"Please tell me you don't believe in ghosts."

"I . . . didn't—"

"Give me a break." Still, Kathy admitted to herself, what had occurred was—so far—unexplainable.

"Okay," Pete said. "Let's find out. We're going in there."

Kathy turned a critical eye toward her brother. "'*We're* going in there.' Who is this 'we' you're referring to?"

"You and me, of course," Pete replied with a devilish grin. "If that glass hatch is unlocked, we've got an open invitation."

"I was afraid you'd say that."

"It's now or never."

"Personally, I think you're cra—"

Pete—ever the impulsive one of the pair who often moved too fast and talked too soon—didn't care. He leaped to his feet, raced out from behind the tree line, and scaled a hedge. He glanced back once, noting with satisfaction that Kathy was shadowing him. Their target, the yellowed glass hatch on the south side of the mansion, lay dead ahead.

What had replaced the old coal chute *under* the grimy glass relic they hadn't a clue. They had forgotten to ask Roberta about that, but it made no difference. The game plan was to gain access to the manor house, which had proved elusive. Until now. Maybe.

Pete reached the target, falling to his knees and breathing hard —not from fear, but from the frenzy of excitement. *Is this fun, or what?* He grasped hold of a rusty metal handle centered atop the hatch. "Here's hoping," he muttered.

Kathy stood behind him, clasping her hands together, whispering, "Not liking this. Just saying. There's someone in there."

Pete pulled on the handle. *Nothing.* He pulled harder. *Still nada.* He stood and, grabbing it again with both hands, fiercely determined, yanked hard, twisting his body more than halfway around in the effort. *Click!*

"Oh, Lord," Kathy muttered.

As Pete swung the hatch high enough to squeeze under, its hinges squealed with a mournful sound.

"Pete, you'll wake the dead," Kathy hissed.

"Stairs," he breathed. "Go down the stairs, Kathy."

"Me?" She glanced downward into near pitch darkness. Moonlight exposed the first two or three wooden steps, descending at a steep angle before fading into nothingness.

"Yes! Go. Now. This stupid hatch is freaking heavy. Don't worry. I'll be right behind you."

Kathy grasped her brother's shoulder for support and set one foot on the first step. It was solid enough, which seemed oddly comforting. She paused, reaching for the cellphone in her back pocket.

"No flashlight!" Pete warned. "Not until we get down there."

"Who put you in charge?"

"Just do it! My arms are about to fall off."

"You're responsible if I break my neck."

"So noted."

She plunked herself down, sitting on the top step, bumping down one stair at a time, counting twelve before reaching hard, cold concrete under both feet. An awful smell greeted her—stale, moldy, and pervasive. "I'm on the basement floor," she called up, her voice hushed once again. "And it stinks to high heaven down here."

Something unseen scampered along the floor. Kathy wanted to scream as she drew her feet in closer. "There're *rats* down here!"

"You're surprised, after sixty years? I'm not."

"You're a regular genius."

Her brother, silhouetted against the moonlit night sky, twisted his body under the hatch and slipped down the top two stairs in a single step. Then he allowed the ancient relic to close behind him. Gently.

Click.

Kathy's ears perked up. "*Wait!* Did that thing just lock itself?"

Pete pushed up on the hatch, hard. "Well, it's stuck at least. I don't get it. It should open from the inside, but it won't move."

"Oh, Lord," his sister moaned again.

"Not a problem." He negotiated the stairs without a moment's hesitation, springing onto the concrete floor as if it were a basketball court. "Getting out of here will be easier than it was to get in."

"And you know this *how?*"

"That part is still unknown."

"Brilliant."

Kathy fired off a quick text message to the Jackson twins, Suzanne and Tom. Ever since graduating into Prescott High, the Jackson and Brunelli foursome had teamed up to solve mysteries and fight crime. *The Daily Pilot,* Prescott's hometown newspaper, and its star reporter, Heidi Hoover, had covered their cases, regularly plastering them across the front page. It was Heidi—who had soon become a best friend and often a fellow investigator too—who had dubbed the four young sleuths "the mystery searchers." The name had stuck.

Her hurried text read: *It's back! Made it into the mansion—thru the glass hatch.* She hit Send and muted her cell. Kathy knew that the keys to One Wainrich Manor would arrive the following day. *No more crazy stakeouts.* The thought filled her with a transitory moment of joy.

"It sure smells bad down here," Pete grumbled.

"I already told you that."

The siblings tapped the flashlight icons on their cellphones, projecting light that they filtered through their fingers. The beams illuminated a vast basement with a crusty old electric furnace at the center, stone cold. Along one wall stretched a long workbench, three feet deep, littered with rusty hand tools covered in cobwebs. Two additional sets of stairs, widely separated, led up to the main floor, apparently to opposite ends of the house.

"Well, that's weird enough," Kathy whispered.

"What?"

"Two sets of stairs heading up from a basement? Never seen that before."

"Look at the size of this place," Pete mumbled. "It's a *mansion*, remember?"

That made sense. Kind of.

Between the two flights of stairs were four closed doors. At some point, it appeared, the Wainrich family must have divided up the raw basement space.

Pete sidled over to the first door. "Whaddaya think's in here?"

Kathy followed, fighting her trepidation with every step. Her brother pushed open the door and stepped in, projecting light into a tiny bedroom. Inside was a bed covered with a chocolate-colored duvet, a small table and lamp, and a set of half-open dresser drawers that turned out to be full of clothes, all neatly folded. Plus closets, their doors splayed wide open, jam-packed with even more clothing on hangers.

"They left everything behind," Pete murmured.

"Uh-huh. Just like Roberta said." Kathy ran a finger across the top of the dresser to find dust a quarter inch thick. *E-e-e-ew.*

"What's behind door number two, I wonder?" Pete joked.

"Very funny, I'm sure."

Opening all the remaining doors one by one revealed a small

bathroom with a shower stall—no tub—and two additional bedrooms. All very neat and all *very* dusty. They closed the door of the third bedroom and stood outside on the basement floor.

"Why would a rich family build three bedrooms in this yucky basement?" Kathy asked. "There must be enough *nice* bedrooms upstairs. The kind with windows—sunlight, fresh air, little things like that."

"They probably had lots of company," Pete said, his voice low. "But imagine: the Wainrich family departed more than half a century ago, leaving the mansion and all this stuff to rot away. I'm surprised that—"

Somewhere in the manor, they heard the distinct sound of a door squeaking on its hinges. "What was *that?*" Kathy asked, almost gagging on her words.

"We've got company," Pete whispered. His jaw slackened.

They killed their phone flashlights, plunging themselves into total darkness.

"We're not alone, are we?" Kathy hissed. "We never were."

Worse, retreating through the glass hatch wasn't an option. To escape, they would have to access the manor's first floor, and even then . . .

"Weird, huh?"

"No fooling. How are we gonna get out of here?"

"Who's leaving?" Pete replied. Nothing much ever seemed to bother her brother, except confined spaces, which could make him panic, and being hugged, which he basically hated. "We're here to find out who—or what—is haunting this mansion. Now we're in. Follow me."

"Follow you? I can't even *see* you."

"Just stay close. I'm heading over to the stairs."

With only his feet and outstretched hands to guide him, Pete glided across the concrete floor, silent as the proverbial grave. Kathy hesitated, listening for him—*He's so quiet*—before setting off

7

for the closer of the two sets of stairs. She began negotiating them one step at a time. Pete had to be somewhere in front, she figured. She counted sixteen steps up before her nose bumped into a—

Door?

"Pete! Where *are* you?" she called out in an urgent whisper.

"Right here," he replied. From the far, far side of the basement.

"Tell me you're not serious. *You're at the wrong door—*"

"You're on the wrong set of stairs!"

At that second, a clock—it must have been huge, a tall grandfather clock maybe—chimed from somewhere within the mansion. The sound resonated, deep and jarring, down into the basement. *Bong . . . bong . . . bong . . . bong . . .*

Kathy's hand flew to her mouth.

Bong . . . bong . . . bong . . . bong . . .

Her mind raced. *How could a clock left unwound for six decades be chiming?* What the heck!

Bong . . . bong . . . bong . . . bong . . .

Midnight! Whispering no longer seemed viable. "We gotta get out of here!" she called out.

"Go through the door," Pete said in a rush. "Turn left. I'll be there."

She choked out the words. "Are we—are you *sure?*"

"Trust me! I'm heading onto the main floor. Now! You do the same."

Kathy grasped the doorknob and turned it ever so slowly. Then she pulled, cracking the door open a couple of inches. It creaked. She angled her head and peeked through the narrow opening. Too dark to see a thing. She opened it wider, and took one cautious step in . . .

Something moved.

2

HAPPY BIRTHDAY!

Four days earlier, a Wednesday, December 28, just after 7:00 p.m.

"*. . . Happy birthday to you-u-u-u!*" The Jackson and Brunelli families finished up their traditional birthday song to the Chief. Applause and a burst of joyful laughter rang out. The guest of honor stood, raising his glass to everyone in thanks. Other diners in the Hassayampa Inn's Peacock Room, the Chief's favorite restaurant, had joined in the celebratory song. So had a lady sitting by herself close to the street-side windows.

"Thank you so much," the Chief said, glancing around the dining room. He smiled and waved to everyone before sitting back down.

The lone woman had arrived just after the birthday group seated themselves. Suzanne and Kathy couldn't help noticing the strikingly elegant figure, somewhere in her seventies, on the short side, with pure white hair, conservatively dressed for a night out— as the hostess led her to a table for two. Later, they had exchanged looks when she ordered—for one. She sat alone, treating herself to one of the chef's most prized entrées: baked salmon with lemon-caper sauce, together with a glass of white wine.

Later, as the Jackson-Brunelli party's server, Sam, was slicing the enormous birthday cake that Sherri, the twins' mother, had discreetly ordered in advance, Suzanne whispered something to him. Then she stood and walked over to the lone lady's table.

The tall, willowy girl with shoulder-length auburn hair stopped in front of her. "Ma'am, thank you *so* much for joining in the birthday song for my father. My name is Suzanne Jackson. Would you care to join us for cake? We have plenty to share."

"Oh, my dear, that's so *nice* of you." A smile lit up the lady's face as she stood. "Of course, I would be delighted." She reached down, picked up a giant black purse, and followed Suzanne back to the table.

"Everybody," Suzanne said, "this is—"

"Mrs. Roberta Robertson, and please, my friends call me Roberta."

Suzanne smiled. "Mrs. Robertson—*Roberta*—will join us for birthday cake."

A round of "Hello!" and "Welcome!" circled the table.

Kathy stood and shook hands with Roberta, introducing herself. "I'm Kathy Brunelli, Suzanne's best friend, and it's wonderful to meet you. This is my brother, Pete—

Pete sprang to his feet. "Pleased to meet you, ma'am," he said, grabbing a chair from an adjacent empty table and offering it gallantly to Roberta. The two girls made room for her between them. "And this is my best friend, Tom," he added.

Tom smiled and shook hands with the families' new guest. "My pleasure, Roberta. Would you care for coffee?"

"Thank you. No coffee, dear. But I will have a cup of tea if that's possible."

"It sure is," Tom answered. He waved to their server. "Sam, could you please arrange some tea for the lady?"

Roberta looked at Tom and Suzanne and shook her head. "My, it's remarkable how you look so much alike. Are you twins?"

"We are," Suzanne said, "and I'm the older—."

"By five whole minutes!" Tom quipped.

"And wiser one," his sister finished with a grin.

Roberta laughed, a pleasant ringing sound that compelled everyone at the table to smile. She seemed to have a wonderful sense of humor. "Kathy," she asked, "are you and Pete twins, as well?"

"No, but many people think we are. It's our Italian heritage. Same complexion, same black hair, even the same height."

"Her nose is bigger," Pete pointed out.

Kathy winked at Roberta. "So is his mouth." She was a vivacious, natural-born comic, her quick sense of humor a gift from her mother.

More introductions followed as Roberta met Joe and Maria, Pete and Kathy's parents. Sherri, the twins' mother, arose from the far end of the table. She walked over to shake hands with the lady, her husband in tow.

"Hi, I'm Sherri, the twins' mother. And this is the birthday boy," she said, giving her husband a hug, "Chief Edward Jackson."

"Oh, my word." Roberta's hand flew to her mouth. "Are you Prescott's chief of police?"

"Indeed I am." The Chief had grown accustomed to the public's typical reaction upon meeting him for the first time. His sterling reputation in the community always preceded him. "And I am very pleased to make your acquaintance."

"So that means," she said, breaking eye contact with him and gazing around the table, "that you four must be . . . the mystery searchers."

Pete did his best to stifle a grin. He secretly loved it when people recognized them. "Yes, we sure are."

Roberta leaned forward, as if she were about to share a secret, her eyes scanning their faces. *"How wonderful.* I've been wanting to talk to you."

Suzanne sat back in surprise. "You have? Whatever for?"

Just then, Sam arrived with a small pot of tea, a teacup and saucer, and a glass of water for the older lady. He poured the tea for her. "Thank you so much," she said politely. She stopped to add milk and two teaspoons of sugar, stirring the concoction before looking up again. "What I'm going to reveal will sound rather strange. I don't want you to think I'm a batty old lady. Tell me you'll listen."

"You have our undivided attention," Kathy said.

Sam and another server swept around the table, distributing nine plates of chocolate cake. It took only minutes for the desert to disappear. Kathy ate half of hers before shoveling the balance over to Pete. "He's a human garbage can," she whispered to Roberta.

"How'd you like it, Dad?" Tom asked.

"Great, best ever." As a rule, the Chief avoided desserts. He worked hard at trying to stay in shape.

"This cake is delicious," Roberta commented. She took another sip of her cooling tea. "I can't thank you enough." She glanced around at the foursome. "Have you ever heard of Wainrich Manor?"

"Oh, sure," Suzanne answered. "It's that little cul-de-sac that backs up to Pegasus Point Drive, right?"

"In the southeast corner of the city," Pete said. "There're like, uh, three or four old Victorian-style homes in there."

"Three," Roberta said, catching Pete's eye. "One of them is mine."

"That's where you live?" The houses on Wainrich Manor were, Pete knew, quite large.

The twins noticed their father had sat bolt upright, his eyes fixed on Roberta.

"Yes. It belonged to my grandfather. He left it to my father, and

I inherited it two decades ago." She didn't realize it, but the entire table was now hanging on her every word.

"You live there by yourself?" Suzanne asked.

"Yes, I do." She paused, looking away for a few seconds. "Ever since my husband passed a few years ago."

Soon enough, the Peacock Room emptied out; the birthday group had it to themselves. The sounds of dishes being cleared in the kitchen drifted into the dining room.

"I'm spoiling your party," Roberta said, glancing around at everyone. "I'm sorry. That wasn't my intention."

The Chief spoke up from the end of the table. "Please, go ahead. We've had lots of fun tonight. We're all interested in what you have to say."

"Well, it started two nights ago. And I have to admit, it *is* on the weird side. In fact, my neighbor, Brenda, just packed up her family and moved to Phoenix—this morning. At least until this thing is over."

"What thing?" Kathy said.

"Something I never expected to see," Roberta declared. She leaned forward to rest both elbows on the table and folded her hands together. "A flickering light appeared in One Wainrich Manor. It's a mansion—the biggest one of the three by far, abandoned now for sixty years. Two nights ago, a light showed up from nowhere, moving around inside, from floor to floor—*at midnight*."

3

THE FLICKERING LIGHT

No one uttered a word. Roberta sat back in her chair and took a deep breath. She drank a few sips of cold water before continuing.

"You might wonder what that means. I sure do. But allow me to provide you with some perspective. When you arrive at our cul-de-sac, you'll see three homes. Mine is on the left, Two Wainrich Manor, a beautiful old home sitting on an acre of land. I grew up in that house. And today, after all these years, I still love it."

She stopped again, seeming to gather her thoughts. "Across the cul-de-sac from me is Three Wainrich Manor. That belonged to the Foley family. Their kids were all friends of mine growing up, especially Claudine, Brenda's mother." She looked wistful. "Claudine and her husband passed years ago—today it's Brenda's home. Brenda McGregor, now—that's her married name. To see it sitting empty is quite sad."

"What caused Brenda and her family to move away?" Sherri asked.

"The flickering light frightened her nearly to death."

"'A flickering light,'" Suzanne repeated. The hair had risen on the back of her neck. "Please explain. *What is it?*"

"I wish I knew. Two nights ago, Brenda called me, waking me up around midnight. At first, I figured she must have been dreaming. As I mentioned, One Wainrich Manor has been vacant for six decades. That's the one between our two homes, but farther in, at the end of the cul-de-sac. It backs up to the red rocks, the nicest property by far. And the largest of the three too. I played there as a youngster—me, Claudine, and Dorothy Wainrich. We were best friends and forever intriguing . . . pretending we were three damsels in distress, or three explorers on a safari. The giant veranda out front was a favorite playground. The house was so big you could get lost in it. In fact, I did!"

"You got lost in the house?" Maria asked.

"Oh, yes. When I was about four. Somehow, the other kids left me by myself on the third floor. I don't think I'd ever been upstairs before. There are two sets of stairwells, mirroring each other - one toward the front and the other toward the back of the house. They go from the third floor straight down to the basement. I walked down one set of stairs—the one closer to the front of the mansion —from top to bottom. But the basement doors wouldn't budge when I tried to return, so I sat down and waited. Pretty soon, everyone came looking for me." She smiled. "Dorothy's grandfather, Mr. Wainrich, found me. I had been crying, and he picked me up and held me. I remember that day like it was yesterday, all these years later."

"Who *was* Mr. Wainrich?" Pete asked.

"Rupert Wainrich was one of the city's leading citizens," Roberta replied, almost with a hint of pride. "And truly a nice man." She stopped to pour more tea for herself. "Of course, you're familiar with the Yavapai County Courthouse?"

"Sure. That's where *we* played when we were kids," Kathy

answered. "On the grounds outside. And we solved a case there a while back too."

"I know, I read about that mystery in the *Pilot*," Roberta replied. "And I used to play there myself." She reached over and squeezed Kathy's hand. "Wonderful memories, aren't they, dear? Anyway, they built that courthouse from handsome granite quarried right here in Prescott. Guess who owned the quarry?"

"Mr. Wainrich," Tom said.

"Close enough. Rupert's father, Eldon, in fact. After Prescott's great fire of nineteen hundred, Eldon rebuilt many of the downtown buildings. That was long before Rupert's time. Years passed before he took over. Then he ran the family construction company for nigh on sixty-five years. And he was just as successful as his father."

She took another sip of tea. "Rupert developed the cul-de-sac and built those three houses. The Victoria era had long passed, but he looked on them as a work of art. He forged ahead, building *his* home—One Wainrich Manor—larger than the other two. The thing was so big that all the kids called it the Wainrich *mansion.*"

Her eyes glistened. She dug out a tissue from her purse and dabbed them. "Then, one day, our entire world turned upside down. Dorothy and her brother, William—everyone called him Bill when he was little—and their mother, Hilda, lived with Rupert and his wife, Barbara, Hilda's parents. The Wainriches were very doting grandparents. But that summer, Hilda took Dorothy and Bill to spend the summer vacation with their paternal grandparents—her deceased husband's parents—in New Hampshire. It seemed the mansion was to undergo a major renovation. I missed Dorothy terribly—she didn't return until a week or two before school began. It was the longest summer of my life."

She paused again, just for a few seconds, and blew her nose. "Days later, Rupert's wife, Barbara, passed away after a terrible car accident. We all loved her dearly. It was the biggest funeral the city had ever witnessed. And then—"

"Rupert Wainrich disappeared," the Chief cut in with a leaden voice. "Just five days later. Never to be seen again."

Silence shrouded the dining room. No one seemed to know what to say. Roberta stared at the Chief with an intense, penetrating gaze of sadness. Seconds passed. "Yes, sir. I see you're well versed in the family history."

"I am," the Chief replied. "Although it was long before my time. Rupert Wainrich is still on our books as a missing person, a cold case. Back then, Prescott City Police developed a theory that Mr. Wainrich must have had a complete breakdown of some kind— total amnesia, forgot his own identity, got lost somehow. That was the best they could come up with."

"A missing person," Roberta whispered, almost to herself, blinking away a tear. "Yes. Over time, we heard many theories about his disappearance, none of which panned out. Today he'd be well over a hundred years old. We may never learn what happened to him, but life changed on Wainrich Manor that summer . . . forever."

Her voice caught. A tear fell down one cheek, only to be wiped away from a tissue that magically appeared in her hand. "Nothing was ever the same again."

"Tell us about the flickering light," Suzanne prompted gently.

"Oh, yes, I'm sorry. I got carried away. Well, Brenda called me close to midnight on Tuesday. I didn't know *what* was happening. She and her husband had come home from a late-night social gathering. A retirement party, I believe. She said, 'Roberta, I swear a strange light's moving around inside the mansion. On the third floor, and it's frightening me.' I pooh-poohed her, of course—in fact, I told her she was nuts. But she beseeched me to meet her out front. So I threw a jacket over my housecoat and walked out into the freezing cold. Brenda stood in the center of the cul-de-sac, staring hard at Number One. I hurried over and joined her. Guess what?"

"No light?" Kathy guessed.

"Yes, at first," she replied. "But no sooner did I tell Brenda that she'd been seeing things than 'it' glowed up on the third floor. *Right in front of our eyes.* I darn near passed out. And, of course, Brenda panicked like nothing I'd ever seen, and for good reason. I mean, someone wandering around the mansion sixty years later? Well, that's plain crazy. Next thing we know, the light faded away."

The elegant lady stopped, picked up her fork, and ate a last little morsel of leftover cake. "This is awfully good," she said, gazing toward the Chief. "You're a very lucky man, sir."

"Yes, I am," he replied with a half-smile.

"What happened next?" Pete asked impatiently.

"The floating light reappeared after a few moments on the second floor. Then it vanished again. That did it for Brenda. She left me standing by myself. I mean—I'm not kidding—she ran straight into Number Three and slammed the front door shut." She shook her head, but the corners of her mouth turned up. "Locked it too. But I don't scare easily. So I walked over to Number One to check the strange phenomenon from up close. Pretty soon, it glowed up again, this time in the basement, before fading away. *Gone.*"

"That's where you spotted it last?" Joe asked.

"The mansion doesn't have basement windows, but there's an old coal chute still covered by its original glass hatch on the south side. As I approached the house there, the light moved underneath the hatch. I stood above it and watched, transfixed. You can't see through it clearly—the glass is filthy and badly pitted. The glow appeared beneath it as a soft, flickering blur."

"Weren't you frightened?" Sherri asked.

"Fascinated, not frightened." Roberta smiled. "I don't believe in ghosts. I wondered, *What the heck is it, and why is it here?*"

Suzanne sat back in her chair. "Did you figure it out?"

"No, nor last night, either."

"It came back?" Joe asked.

Maria and Sherri exchanged a look.

"Yes, indeed. It intrigued me so much that the very next night—yesterday evening—I parked myself on my veranda. Starting at eleven-thirty p.m. There's a straight-line view from there to the facade of Number One. I wore an oversize winter jacket to keep warm and brought out a thermos of hot chamomile tea. The thing glowed up at midnight, this time appearing first on the *second* floor before heading upstairs. I made the mistake of phoning Brenda and getting her out of bed. She caught sight of it on the third floor just before it snuffed itself out."

"That did it for her," Maria surmised.

"It sure did," Roberta said. "It *is* strange. That's why she took her family this morning and fled to Phoenix. And to be honest, it's the reason I came out for dinner tonight. I needed to get some feeling of normality back into my life. Brenda says One Wainrich Manor is haunted, and she's not returning unless—*and until*—the thing departs. Forever. And she's serious too."

"Haunted!" Kathy exclaimed. An involuntary shiver ran up and down her spine.

"Dang," Pete muttered to no one in particular, thinking *all the while, I can't wait.*

"Did you consider calling the police?" the Chief probed.

"Yes, sir," Roberta replied. "I also considered they wouldn't believe me."

"Who do you think it could be?" Tom asked.

"Me? I haven't a clue. It is quite mysterious. But there's no doubt in Brenda's mind. She says the ghost of Rupert Wainrich has returned."

4

THE WAINRICH FAMILY

It snowed early Thursday morning, a soft shower of flurries that faded away by daybreak. A thin veil of powdery whiteness, slippery roadways, and dark, threatening skies covered the city. The Brunelli siblings drove over to the Jacksons' house after breakfast. The foursome, out for their Christmas break, had another week to go.

"Heh-heh," Pete chuckled as he stuck his head into the refrigerator. "You know that lady could just be yanking our chain, right?" Finding nothing of interest to snack on, he settled for a cup of coffee, adding a splash of cream and three teaspoons of sugar. Then he slurped out loud, all to a look of disdain from his sister.

Suzanne disagreed. "That lady has a name, and it's Roberta. And Roberta's one of the nicest and most sincere people we've ever met. If she says there's a flickering light coming and going, I believe her."

"I'm with you," Kathy declared, siding with her best friend. "She's quite the elegant lady too."

Pete snorted. "What's that got to do with anything?"

"Stay tuned," his sister shot back. "You'll figure it out."

Tom—the mystery searchers' high-tech guy—grinned. Quiet and thoughtful, he had learned to code in grade school and had become a founding member of Prescott High's prestigious technology club in his freshman year. "Sorry, bro. I'm siding with the girls this time around. Roberta's for real, even if her friend Brenda might be a little goofy. Remember, she's the one the flickering light drove right out of her home. She upped and moved her family to Phoenix. Just 'cause of a *light*."

"Well . . ." Pete hesitated. "True enough, I guess. My bad. Okay, I'm in. Game on! So what's the deal with the weird light?"

"Not what," Suzanne said. *"Who."*

"Roberta said Dorothy's family abandoned the mansion sixty years ago," Kathy reminded her. "So if it's a 'who,' how did they get inside?"

"Exactly!" Tom thought out loud. *"Somebody* has to be responsible for it."

"Could be a ghost," Pete said, grinning, "carrying a candle."

His sister glared at him. "Oh, please."

"Just saying."

"Don't."

"It really *could* be an 'it,'" Tom said. "some kind of remote-controlled device—a miniature drone with a prop lantern attached, something like that."

"Hmph," Kathy grunted.

Tom searched for a reason, a clue, a way in to the mystery. "We need to know more about the Wainrich family. Rupert's wife died in a terrible accident, and he vanished five days later. Roberta said that as a child she played with Dorothy Wainrich. What happened to her? If she's still alive, where is she?"

Kathy recalled Roberta's words. "And Dorothy had a brother. Where is he? And who owns the mansion today?"

Pete added more sugar to his coffee. "Roberta should have answers to all those questions."

THE HAUNTING OF WAINRICH MANOR

"Let's split into teams," Suzanne suggested. "Kathy and I will go say hello to Roberta. You guys check out the archives at *The Daily Pilot.* Rupert Wainrich was a local leader. There's gotta be a treasure trove of historical info about him—and his family."

Pete reached for his cellphone. "I'll call Heidi."

THE BOYS DROVE DOWNTOWN TO THE OFFICES OF *THE DAILY PILOT.* Heidi Hoover met them in the entrance and led the way through a maze of corridors. The diminutive star reporter had been the editor-in-chief of Prescott High's student paper in her senior year, just as the foursome began junior high.

"All right," she said as they stepped into the central archival room. "What's up?" Heidi, known for her rapid-fire way of speaking, seldom wasted words.

The boys summed up their latest mystery. In conclusion, Tom mentioned Brenda's claim that One Wainrich Manor had become "haunted." That sent Heidi into gales of laughter, her tight black curls bouncing around her head. "*Haunted?* That's awfully funny, right?"

Pete grinned. "I'm with you, Heidi."

"I dunno," Tom said. "It's a strange one. It drove the poor neighbor lady and her family out of the city—within forty-eight hours! They moved to Phoenix."

That gave Heidi pause. "Wow... *seriously?*"

"Yup."

"Well, maybe there's a story here. You guys remember how to access the archive?"

"Sure do."

"It's all yours. Have at it. Call me if you find anything interesting."

The newspaper had been in operation since 1881. The resident archivists stored much of its newer material in digital form, but the earlier years' editions were accessible only on microfilm: the bound volumes of the older issues had all been printed on high-acid newsprint. They were too fragile to examine.

Each story was tagged with searchable keywords. Key in the appropriate term and the desktop screen would display specific headlines along with matching dates. For pre-2000 stories, each day's entire edition was stored on a single microfilm kept in rows of metal bins. A researcher would load the film into a reader and scan to the correct page number.

"Think about it," Pete said, typing in *Rupert Wainrich*. "This guy was a town leader. I'll bet there's a lot—"

"*Crud!*" Tom exclaimed. The boys stared at the screen, dumb-founded. "Is there ever. Three-hundred-and-eighty mentions . . . each one with a date, section, and page reference. You've gotta be kidding!"

Pete sucked in air. "We'll be here for *days.*"

———

Suzanne turned into Wainrich Manor and brought the Chevy to a halt. To their left appeared Roberta's Victorian-style house—Two Wainrich Manor—a handsome three-story, standing on extensive grounds blanketed by a thin veil of snow, with a gravel driveway leading to a closed double garage.

Kathy stared, dumbstruck. "My gosh, that place is *gorgeous.*"

"All three of them are. You can tell they built them at the same time."

"That's Brenda's home to the right," Kathy said, pointing. "Number Three. It's a carbon-copy of Roberta's house. But it needs a little work."

"Roberta said Brenda's got a whole passel of kids. That could explain it. She has priorities other than home renovation."

"Take a peek at the mansion," Kathy said, staring straight ahead. The abandoned One Wainrich Manor was a majestic Victorian Revival–style house with a steeply pitched roof punctuated by dormer windows, a wide porch, bay windows on the ground floor, towers, and overhangs. Surrounded by a three-foot hedge with a meager covering of snow, the house dominated a wide lot, bordered in the rear by barren oaks and gigantic red rocks.

Suzanne said, "It's rather lonely looking, isn't it?"

"Uh-huh. No wonder. Sixty years is a long time. It sure needs a paint job."

"That's a fact. And check out the size of it. I'll bet it's larger by half than the other two. No wonder the kids called it a mansion." She pulled the Chevy onto Roberta's empty driveway, tires crunching over the gravel. "Ready?"

Roberta answered their ring with a cheerful smile. "Come in," she greeted them through the screen door. "I've been baking cookies ever since you phoned."

The girls stepped into a spacious hallway. Roberta refused to shake hands, instead hugging both. "I'm so happy you came," she said, leading them into a living room that overlooked the cul-de-sac. The room featured upholstered period furniture, formal and ornate with dark, rich colors and heavy tapestries. Suzanne thought that she had never seen a living room as beautiful.

"Please make yourself comfortable," Roberta said with a smile. "You didn't think I was batty, after all."

Kathy shook her head. "No, Roberta, we sure didn't. We're committed to helping you, but we have questions."

"Well, I hope I have answers." She laughed again. Roberta, they realized, had a personality that lit up everyone around her. "I have water, coffee, tea, and homemade shortbread cookies. What would you like?"

Fifteen minutes later, with refills of coffee to wash down the delicious cookies, the girls got down to business.

"Tell us more about the Wainrich family," Suzanne urged.

"I could spend days telling you about them," Roberta said. She set both hands in her lap. "What do you want to know?"

"What happened to your friend, Dorothy Wainrich?" Suzanne asked. "Is she still around?"

"Oh, my goodness," Roberta said with a deep sigh. She closed her eyes for a few seconds to compose herself. "Well, I told you about Rupert Wainrich, how successful he was. A delightful man, I might add. He and his wife Barbara had just the one child, Hilda. She married, but her husband died young, leaving her with two kids—Dorothy, one of my best friends, as I've told you, and her younger brother, Bill. Those two fought like cats and dogs—a never-ending battle. They lived in the mansion with their mom and grandparents."

"Dorothy was your age?" Kathy asked.

"Yes. We were inseparable and shared birthdays a week apart. Bill was four years younger. The years flew by. Before we knew it, Dorothy and I began our first year at Prescott High. That's when everything fell apart."

She stood, stepped over to the fireplace, and picked up a framed four-by-six photograph of two girls, arm in arm with books at their feet, their faces shining with happiness and excitement. She held the picture out toward Suzanne and Kathy. "This is Dorothy and me, taken on the morning of our first day at Prescott High. My mother took the photo. Isn't Dorothy a distinctive-looking person? Those high cheekbones ran through the entire family. Everyone thought she was so pretty."

"Oh my gosh," Kathy murmured. "She surely was."

"You both were," Suzanne said.

"Well, thank you, dear." Roberta sat back down and continued. "Hilda's mother died in that terrible accident a week later. Five days after, her father disappeared. And the following month, Hilda deserted the mansion. She loaded up the station wagon, drove off, and never looked back. She felt her father had abandoned her and his grandchildren in the darkest moment of their lives. So she dragged Dorothy and Bill off to Atlanta and started life over. I don't know why she chose Atlanta. It was one of the saddest days of my life. Hilda passed away unexpectedly just a few years later. Dorothy was in her fourth year in college, and Bill had joined the military."

Suzanne asked, "Why is the mansion sitting there empty?"

"Because Dorothy is the spitting image of her mother in every way." A rare frown had crossed Roberta's face. "She refuses to face the past and, at the same time, won't let it go. So she lives in Atlanta by herself but pays the taxes and basic maintenance on Number One. For many years, she kept paying the electric bills too and kept the thermostat set to protect the house from cold in winter and heat in summer. But she had the power cut off long ago. The mansion just sits there, cold and dark, slowly rotting away."

"'Basic maintenance,'" Kathy repeated. "Like what?"

"Care of the grounds, for the most part. The owners of all three houses share the salary of Henry Travers. In the summer, he looks after the landscaping. Cuts the lawns, trims the trees, rakes the leaves, paints the fences, stuff like that. In the winter, we'll get the odd heavy snow. These old roofs can only take so much weight, so he'll clear off the snow and shovel the sidewalks and driveways. Dorothy still sends Henry a check each month."

"Are you in touch with Dorothy?"

"Until ten years ago, yes. Then she stopped writing. I send her a Christmas card each year, but that's it. She never replies and refuses to answer my telephone calls. I reach out once a year, but..."

"What about Bill?"

"After graduating from high school, he joined the Navy. That's the last anyone heard of him. Dorothy wouldn't ever talk about him—she believes Bill abandoned her too. It seemed they had one last fight, and it must have been a dilly. He told her he never wanted to see her again. She claims it runs in the family. They inherited equal shares in the property, but Dorothy has been solely responsible for it ever since Bill disappeared. Years ago, I wrote to the Navy, asking for a copy of Bill's service record. They refused my request because I'm not family."

"Does Dorothy ever visit?"

"Not once in sixty years."

5

THE MANSION

As Tom and Pete dug into the hundreds of search results for *Rupert Wainrich,* they found to their relief that many of the news stories weren't about him at all.

"Check it out," Tom said. "They recorded his name on every vote he cast as a member of city council over a ten-year period. Narrow it down by keying in *Rupert Wainrich missing* and see what we get."

"Copy that," Pete said. *Tap—tap—tap.* "Wow. Eighty-seven articles. That helps. And they range over a twenty-five-year period." He clicked on the last one. "This is an anniversary story about the day he vanished a quarter century earlier. Says the police never came up with a decent lead."

"Let's go back to the beginning," Tom suggested.

A minute later, Pete exclaimed, "Eureka! Two days after he disappeared, and the news made the front page." The headline reads, "Rupert Wainrich missing."

Tom dug out the film and loaded it into a reader. Beside the headline was a giant black-and-white photo of Mr. Wainrich. He had eyes like an eagle, high cheekbones, and pure white hair combed straight back. The head-and-shoulders shot showed him in an expensive-looking suit jacket and tie.

"There's a subhead," Tom said, reading out loud: "'Search for town leader widens.'" He continued: "Rupert Wainrich, Prescott business leader and longtime city councilman, disappeared from his home sometime early on Sunday morning. His daughter, Dorothy, reported him missing later the same day. Prescott City Police are asking for the public's help. At a press conference yesterday, Police Chief Warren Hatcher stated, 'We've turned the house upside down and there's no sign of Mr. Wainrich. His car is still in the garage. We checked bus, train, and airport departures and came up empty. I've alerted police forces throughout Arizona. Right now, we have no leads.' Five days earlier, Mr. Wainrich had attended Prescott's largest funeral. His wife, the well-known socialite Barbara Wainrich, had died in a tragic car accident."

"You know what they're hinting at, right?" Tom asked, glancing over to Pete.

"Uh-huh. That he simply took off for parts unknown. But there's an immense hole in that theory."

"There sure is. No one ever saw him again. Remember, the Chief mentioned he's still listed as a missing person."

Pete grimaced. "Still *missing*, but a living *person* no longer. This dude would be well over a century old."

"Which explains why Brenda believes in the haunting of One Wainrich Manor."

"Uh-huh, by the ghost of Rupert W. Hey, so this Warren Hatcher guy was one of your dad's predecessors."

"Yup, long before. I've heard his name mentioned," Tom said. "There's a picture of him hanging in the hallway at police head-quarters. Look for the funeral notices for Barbara Wainrich . . . see if we can find family pictures."

They did. One photo printed after Barbara's death showed Mr. Wainrich standing beside his daughter, Hilda Wainrich Chase, as he held hands with his grandchildren, William and Dorothy. "Wow," Pete said. "Grim faces—that's tough."

The family resemblance shared by grandfather and grandchildren was quite remarkable.

The stories kept coming. Over the following month, *The Daily Pilot* featured interviews and press conferences with Hilda. In one article, she defended her father, claiming, "He would never just disappear if he were in his right mind."

The boys also found a story titled, "An interview with the Chief," that focused on the continuing search. By then, the business leader had been missing for six months. A reporter asked, "Does Prescott City Police have a theory regarding the disappearance of Rupert Wainrich?" The chief of police replied, "We all know Rupert, of course. Yes, he was very distraught over Barbara's unfortunate accident, but he had a close and loving family and a deep religious faith. We believe the man had some kind of breakdown. It's possible that he might not even know who he is."

Soon, the continuing investigation began shifting from the front page to page three. From there to page ten. And in the end, to anniversaries. Five years. Ten years. Twenty. Twenty-five. Over time, the newspaper buried the sad tale of the Wainrich clan deep into its back pages.

"And then . . . nothing," Pete said.

Tom printed out black-and-white photos of the family members. "Okay, let's go."

AFTER THE BOYS ARRIVED AT ROBERTA'S, AND PETE ELUDED HER HUG, the charming lady offered to take the foursome on a walking tour of One Wainrich Manor—from the outside, of course. "Let me get my jacket," she said. "It's quite chilly out there."

Overhead clouds raced by, leaden and still threatening. A

December wind gusted as the group walked to the front of the mansion. They passed through an old, creaking gate, and a break in a hedge topped with patches of white from the recent snowfall. Every step closer seemed to accentuate the mansion's height; as they stood talking, the three-story structure looked immense.

Roberta pointed to a small dormer window projecting from the sloping roof on the third floor, dead center in the facade. "That's where Brenda first spotted the flickering light. By the time I got out to the cul-de-sac, it had disappeared. But we both watched it on the second floor, and then I saw it the basement."

Pete said, "But the next night—"

"It first appeared on the second floor before moving up to the third."

The mansion's veranda was as wide as the house. "My earliest memories are of playing here," Roberta recalled. She stepped over and ran her hand across the cold surface of the balustrade with its gray, peeling paint. "I remember thinking it was *huge,* much larger than ours. Dorothy and I rode our trikes on the veranda. Then the Foleys arrived, and a new girl showed up—Claudine." She smiled. "Three trikes circled here endlessly. The noise must have been deafening! But nothing bothered Mrs. Wainrich. Not one iota. That woman never met a kid she didn't like."

"So you were around five or six by then," Suzanne figured out loud.

"Oh, I imagine so. They were such carefree times. For many years, Dorothy, Claudine, and I were like triplets; you couldn't keep us apart. No one had any idea what lay before us, of course." She sighed. "I guess that was a good thing."

Kathy pointed up at the sturdy doublewide front doors that appeared to be made of solid wood. "I assume they're locked?"

"Oh, yes," Roberta replied. "Locked and bolted. Same with the windows. Dorothy shut the place up tighter than Fort Knox. You need *four* keys total to get in, different sets for front and back.

Many years ago, I asked her, 'What if a fire starts inside?' She brushed it off, saying, 'That's what insurance is for.' Even today, this house is magnificent, isn't it? Let's circle around it."

The breeze kicked up, pushing against them. Suzanne zipped her jacket up tighter, and Kathy crossed her arms for warmth. They made their way to the mansion's south side and halted before the glass hatch.

"In my day, we grew up with coal chutes for heating. A truck pulled up and dumped a load of coal down here. I'm sure this hatch is original; you can't even see through it. On Tuesday night, after Brenda panicked and ran home, I walked over and stood above it. I could see the flickering glow almost touching the glass. Then it receded downward and" —she gestured with one hand— "faded away."

Kathy gulped. The idea sent a chill up her spine again. They reached the back of the house.

"Here," Roberta swept one arm outward, "was Mrs. Wainrich's kitchen garden. Like everything that family did, it was very large and impressive. She grew the most delicious carrots and peas I ever tasted. The four of us had free access to it; we could gorge ourselves anytime we wanted, and we surely did. There was squash, which I never liked as a child. And lettuce, and corn, and...well, just so much, really. She shared it all with the other two families on the Manor. Nothing left of all that now," she concluded sadly, gazing over the frozen yard.

By now, the group stood dead center behind the house. Pete tried the back door. *Locked tight.* Silence had descended as the foursome took in the sight. This wasn't like any ordinary back-yard, they realized. An acre or more of empty land with patches of snow stretched out around them, ending at a natural wall of gigantic red rocks fronted by barren oak trees.

Roberta traced the outline of the yard with an outstretched hand. "This was a gorgeous summer lawn, manicured and maintained by gardeners. Mrs. Wainrich threw the most extravagant parties out here. Cocktails. Croquet. Champagne. A string quartet. And even if my parents weren't present, I was always like family. All the kids would run around and help ourselves to the food. Nobody gave us a second thought."

Tom wandered along the rear wall of the house. Since this side of the mansion was protected from the easterly wind that had kicked up during the recent snowfall, there were no drifts here. The ground was clear. Tom spotted something. He bent down and picked up a shard of what appeared to be window glass. . . about three inches long, ending in a sharp point. He looked up. "Hey, check this out."

"Whatcha' got?" Pete asked.

"Window glass, I think."

Suzanne tilted her head. "What—so what?"

"Look at that window right above us."

Kathy grinned. "No riddles, Tom. What is it?"

"Notice the difference between *that* one"—he pointed up—"and the window to the left?"

Roberta's eyes widened. "The first looks new."

Pete inhaled sharply. "You're on to something, bro. That's how the ghost got *inside*."

"Ghosts don't break windows," Suzanne argued. "People do."

"Better than that," Tom said. "Someone smashed the glass and then *replaced* it. Not something an ordinary thief would do, right?"

"Wait a sec," Kathy said. "We don't think someone's still *in* there . . . do we?"

"Well . . ." Tom hesitated. "Yeah. It's possible."

Pete liked that. "Maybe even probable!"

6

A LATE-NIGHT VISITOR

M inutes later, the group gathered in Roberta's living room. She offered refreshments, of course, much to Pete's delight. He consumed a prodigious amount of her homemade shortbread cookies.

"Whatever you do," Kathy whispered to her brother, "don't slop food on her sofa."

"My goodness," Roberta exclaimed. Her eyes widened as she watched Pete stuff himself. "Didn't anyone feed you today?"

That threw everyone into gales of laughter. "Not enough," he replied with a grin.

A clue had surfaced, always an exciting event for the mystery searchers. Who had smashed the back window? And then *replaced* it? And why?

"To gain access, of course," Pete said. "What I don't get is the flickering light. I mean, that part drives me crazy."

"You're giving up on the ghost?" Kathy teased.

His lips twitched into a smile. "Me? You already told me there's no such thing."

"No matter what," Tom said, "it's weird."

"Talking weird," Suzanne said, "do you really think someone's in there *right now?*"

"I do," Pete replied.

"If so, he could have seen us poking around," Suzanne said.

"'He'—or 'she'?" Kathy asked.

"Whoever," Pete grunted. "Someone has access and can come and go at will."

Roberta sat back, obviously enjoying herself. Suzanne caught her eye. "Aside from the vanishing of Rupert Wainrich, is there *anything* else in the mansion's history that would attract someone's attention? Were there any robberies in the past, or even a mysterious death?"

"Oh, goodness, no," Roberta replied, shaking her head. "If anything like that had ever happened, I'd know about it."

"First things first," Tom said. "We have to get into the mansion. And breaking another window isn't a good idea."

"Dad wouldn't approve," Suzanne said.

"Neither would I," Roberta said. "What's our second choice?"

"A locksmith," Pete said.

"But first, you call Dorothy," Suzanne suggested. "Explain the situation. Ask her to FedEx copies of the keys and we'll all go in together."

Roberta sighed, sounding resigned. "Well, I can give it a shot. But Dorothy never answers her phone. I've called every year for a decade and left messages. Brenda has tried too. No luck. But I'm willing to try."

"Great," Tom said. "Tell her someone's wandering around inside the mansion carrying a flickering light. If that doesn't get her attention, nothing will. Meantime, we'll stake out the property in the evenings to track our ghostly intruder. In teams."

Kathy groaned to herself. She hated stakeouts. Almost as much as snakes.

Pete raised one arm. "Yay!"

Suzanne wrote her cellphone number on a slip of paper. "Just in case, Roberta. Call me anytime."

THE MYSTERY SEARCHERS FLIPPED COINS TO SEE WHO WOULD HANDLE that evening's stakeout. The twins won—"Lost, in my opinion," Kathy declared—and made their way to Wainrich Manor, arriving at 11:30 p.m.

With Roberta's prior permission, they parked the Chevy in her driveway and trekked over to the dark mansion. A gentle snowfall had begun an hour earlier. They had prepared with warm jackets, gloves, scarves, and an old comforter to sit on.

"The best position is out front to the left," Suzanne said, her voice low. She pointed to a line of trees that looking promising. They walked over and found a perfect hiding spot, settling down between two giant oaks.

Time dragged past in slow motion. There were no pedestrians or traffic in the cul-de-sac—no signs of life. "Except for Roberta," Tom said. Behind them—surprisingly, given the last hour, they thought—lights still burned in Number Two.

It seemed like forever before midnight came—and went. *Nothing.* Soon, Suzanne had had enough. "The main attraction is a no-show."

"Let's hang in here for another fifteen minutes," Tom said. "Then we'll call it a night."

They didn't hear Roberta approach until she called out in a soft voice. "Where are you guys? I've brought hot chocolate." She had also lugged along a folding chair and soon made herself quite comfortable, wrapping a blanket around her legs. *Like she's camping out*, Suzanne thought. *And having a great old time.*

Tom grinned in the dark. "Why didn't we think of that?"

The three of them chatted quietly, as the twins enjoyed the

welcome hot drinks. "No return call from Dorothy," Roberta said. "I didn't expect one, but . . . I'd give her one more day."

Tom nodded. "Tomorrow night, it's Pete and Kathy's turn." Minutes later, he glanced at his cellphone. "It's way past midnight. Let's call it a night."

"Goodness," Roberta said. "Is it that late already? I haven't stayed up past twelve in *decades*."

"I'll circle the house one time," Suzanne said, wandering away. Tom folded the chair for Roberta, and the two started walking back.

Suzanne's voice cut into the night. "Tom! Roberta! Look!"

The two spun around and hustled back. "What's up?" Tom asked.

Suzanne stood at the rear of the house with her cellphone flashlight projecting onto the freshly fallen snow. "While we were enjoying ourselves, someone deserted the mansion."

Tom whistled. "Footprints leading *out* from the back door." He tried the door and found it locked tight.

"But none heading back in," Roberta noted. "Isn't that strange?"

"Not really," Suzanne explained. "It started snowing just before we got here. He—or she—must have arrived earlier, then left when there was snow on the ground."

Roberta stared at the footprints. "It certainly isn't a ghost, is it?" she said with a wry chuckle.

"For sure," Suzanne said, laughing too. "Your friend Brenda will be happy about that, Roberta. We should have been watching out back."

"Let's see where the trail leads," Tom urged.

The three hiked out toward the red rocks at the rear of the property. Halfway there, a new impression appeared in the snow. "What is that?" Roberta asked.

Suzanne leaned over to inspect it. "Seems they hauled something out of the mansion. Whatever the object was, it became too heavy to carry any farther. Someone set it down. The object cut through the snow and into the ground. It had to be darn heavy."

"You're right," Tom said. "Then they dragged it along."

"What could it be?" Roberta murmured.

The path led past the sentinel oaks and between two of the giant red rocks. They passed through the narrow gauntlet before exiting the other side. A grassy area about six feet wide, bordered by a sidewalk, ran parallel to a two-lane paved roadway. The snowfall had covered everything with a thin, white layer of snow that displayed a jumble of footprints.

Tom fell to one knee. "He parked here and loaded up." A car passed by, the noise of its tires muted by the snow.

"We've driven down here before," Suzanne said in recognition. "Pegasus Point Drive, right?"

"Yes," Roberta confirmed. "It's a hilly connecting road with houses on the other side."

Tom summed up. "So our mysterious visitor parked, walked in, and removed something from the mansion. Then he returned here and loaded up."

"That explains why the flickering light didn't show," Suzanne said. "He left early."

"Yup," Tom said glumly. "While we camped outside. What isn't explained is, why do anything to attract attention to his presence? I don't get that part."

Suzanne swiveled toward Roberta. "What's in the mansion? I mean, what could someone haul away from there?"

"Everything's in there," she replied.

The twins looked at her. *Everything?*

"Yes. The place is a sixty-year-old museum. Hilda packed some clothes for her and the kids. She locked up, jumped into the car, and drove to Atlanta."

"And never returned," Tom said.

"Never."

A stunned expression crossed Suzanne's face. "You mean . . . furniture, bedding, dishes, silverware . . . all of that stuff . . . *it's all still in there?*"

"Yup. Everything," Roberta declared again. "It's as if the family walked out yesterday."

7

DEPLOYING TECHNOLOGY

On Friday morning, the mystery searchers trooped downtown to police headquarters.

One of their favorite detectives, Detective Joe Ryan, had agreed to a nine o'clock meeting. The twins had known him since childhood, and the foursome had worked with him on a handful of cases. A low-key investigator with a well-deserved reputation for solving crimes, Ryan was often referred to by the Chief as "the best man on the force."

"Work with Joe," the Chief had advised the previous evening. "There are strange things happening at Wainrich Manor. Eventually, you'll need help."

A shortish individual of little hair and few words, the popular detective wore his trademark rumpled suit and scuffed loafers, which always made the foursome smile. "That man only owns one suit," Suzanne had sometimes quipped. "And when you look at him, you'd swear he sleeps in it."

Detective Ryan met the mystery searchers in the lobby. "Well, hello!" he called out, his hand reaching out in greeting. "Good to see y'all again." He spoke with a pronounced East Texas drawl. "Follow me."

They made their way to a conference room in the bowels of police headquarters. Everyone found a seat around an oversize table. Ryan removed a tiny notebook from his shirt pocket and set it before him. He picked up a ballpoint pen.

"How can I help?"

Suzanne opened the conversation. "We're working on a strange case." They quickly brought him up to date on the haunting of One Wainrich Manor.

"I've been in that cul-de-sac," the detective recalled, "quite a few years ago. As a patrol officer, I found a puppy wandering along Pegasus Point Drive. She had a collar on, and I returned her home. The house on the right, if I remember correctly."

"That's the Foleys' place," Kathy said.

"Sure enough, I think that's the name," Detective Ryan said. "The family blew out of Prescott because of the supposed haunting?"

"It's the daughter's house now, but yes, they sure did."

"Y'all been inside the mansion?" he asked.

"We're working on that," Pete replied. They explained the lockdown of Number One, and the wait for copies of Dorothy's keys to show up. And, of course, the shard of glass.

"Obviously, ghosts don't smash windows," Tom observed. "Nor do they leave footprints in the snow. That's why we're here. We'll set up a hidden high-speed camera in the oaks out back." The mystery searchers had used the system on previous cases, auto-uploading images triggered by a motion detector to the Cloud and then downloading them to their cellphones.

"It'll detect movement from up to a hundred feet away," Pete explained. "We can program it to fire off half a dozen frames in rapid succession. Better yet, the camera displays nighttime footage in infrared."

"So if they show," Kathy continued, "we should capture images of our mysterious visitor. But we'll also stake out Pegasus Point Drive in the evenings. We already have evidence that someone parks a car there. If he or she shows, we'll tail the vehicle, but if we get into trouble . . ."

"No problem," the detective said. "I'll back you up. When are you installing the hardware?"

"Today."

EARLIER, THE MYSTERY SEARCHERS HAD CALLED RAY HUNTLEY, THE president of Prescott High's technology club. In the past, they had often borrowed the school's high-tech software and hardware to aid in solving several cases. Ray trusted them to return the equipment in good shape.

Two of their mysteries had ended up with a donor *replacing* hardware stolen or damaged by the perpetrators. In Ray's world, that was better than great. "New equipment!" he exulted. "More advanced too. Love it!" He also questioned the mystery searchers about each case that came along, and this time was no different.

"What's happening?"

"We've got a new case," Kathy replied. "The haunting of a Prescott mansion!"

"Serious?" Ray asked, startled.

Pete grinned. "Isn't it fun? There's something weird going on. We're gonna figure out what."

Ray lived on a ranch north of the city. After carefully packing the hardware in the Mustang's trunk, the foursome beelined back toward town and parked on Pegasus Point Drive. The mansion loomed on the other side of the bordering red rocks.

They checked for new footprints but found none. "Lots of old ones from us mixed in with our uninvited guest," Pete observed. "Let's get moving. We don't want to alert the, uh . . . whatever."

Tom selected a tree that would serve their purpose. He pulled himself up and climbed, searching for a safe resting spot for the camera that offered the right angle of view. Pete dragged the equipment out from the trunk, and the girls passed it up. Then Tom wired the camera into place and wrapped it in white plastic to camouflage it and protect it from snowfall.

The last step was to cut the plastic, allowing the lens to peek out across the backyard. Viewed from the ground, the installation appeared all but invisible: it had the look of a patch of snow in the crook of a branch.

To test the camera's setting, Suzanne walked around between the mansion and the red rocks. The camera fired off bursts of six shots at a time and transferred them instantly to the Cloud. Tom had come to rely on bursts of still photos rather than video footage for this kind of long-term surveillance: they took up so much less valuable memory while still providing the evidence that law enforcement needed. Plus, stills uploaded and downloaded faster. Seconds later, the images arrived on the foursome's cellphones.

"Whoo-hoo!" Suzanne squealed. "I look great, Tom."

Pete opened his mouth but thought better of it.

"Let's get outta here," Kathy said nervously. "The longer we stay, the greater the chance someone will see us."

THAT EVENING, NOT LONG AFTER ELEVEN O'CLOCK, THE TWINS parked a block away on Pegasus Point Drive.

"No fair," Kathy had complained earlier, while they were ironing out the details of the stakeout. "You guys get to sit in comfort with the heat on while we freeze to death."

"We'll switch off every thirty minutes," Suzanne assured her best friend. "Just call when it gets too cold."

"Negative," Pete objected. "I want to see that flickering light. We'll watch the mansion. Call us if the 'visitor' arrives in his car."

Kathy argued, to no avail. "Okay, boy genius," she concluded, "but you owe me—big-time."

But there was no action that evening. No flickering light, no vehicle parking on Pegasus Point Drive. *Nothing.*

Shortly after midnight, they called it a night and headed home.

But an hour later, the camera app erupted on all four cellphones. *Beep-beep, beep-beep, beep-beep.* Suzanne awoke and raced across the hall to find Tom sitting up in bed, half awake and examining the incoming pics.

"Here he is, Suzie," he whispered in a hoarse voice. "It's a man. The guy's heading into the house now. Who is he . . . ?" In the surreal, rainbow-hued infrared pic, they could see a man who appeared to be mature and quite heavy, his back to the camera, hustling toward Number One. He wore what looked like a wide-brimmed hat and a light jacket. His legs appeared short, but his height was hard to judge in the stills.

Kathy texted, *We're on the way.*

Two minutes later, as Suzanne fired up the Chevy, the app triggered once again. *Beep-beep, beep-beep, beep-beep.*

"What the heck?" Tom muttered. *"He's leaving already?"*

Sure enough, the mysterious man had deserted the mansion. Head down, he rushed back to Pegasus Point Drive. Empty-handed too. The camera failed to get a single decent pic of his face, even when he had passed quite close to the hidden device.

"That hat . . ." Tom groaned.

Pete called. "Time out! *We missed him.*"

"We sure did," Suzanne said. "And we didn't even capture a good image of the guy."

"Why?" Kathy demanded in the background, obviously frus-

trated. "Why did he just come and go? And in a big hurry too. He couldn't have been there for more than a minute."

"Could he have seen the camera?" Suzanne wondered aloud.

"Not likely, in the dark," Pete said.

"No clue," Tom replied.

"One thing is clear now," Kathy remarked grimly. "He comes and goes as he pleases. He either has keys from sixty years ago, or he's changed the locks."

8

A RETURN

On Saturday morning, right after breakfast, Suzanne's cellphone buzzed. "Hello."

"Are you sitting down, dear?"

"Oh, hi, Roberta. Is everything okay?"

"Uh-huh. Dorothy called an hour ago."

"Oh, wow!" Suzanne put the call on Speaker.

Roberta sighed. "It was wonderful, but very emotional. I'm quite tired."

"What did she say?"

"After ten years, a lot. But she agreed to send a set of keys. She'll ship them by FedEx two-day delivery today."

Tom chimed in. "Hi, Roberta. I'm on too. She wouldn't ship them overnight?"

"Nope."

Suzanne asked, "I wonder why?"

"Too cheap. She was born that way. Her father was stingy too."

"Does she have any idea who the mysterious guy is?" Tom asked.

"None. She can't figure it out. But this is a wonderful thing."

Suzanne asked, "What do you mean?"

"My oldest friend is talking to me again."

THAT EVENING, THE MYSTERY SEARCHERS WERE IN PLACE BY 11:00 p.m. They agreed to stay past midnight. And they sought Roberta's help.

The Brunellis slouched down in the front seat of their Mustang, hiding in a residential area on the far side of Pegasus Point Drive. Every few minutes, Pete fired up the car and flipped the heat on. The siblings enjoyed an excellent view of the street in both directions. Should the mysterious visitor return, they had two objectives: first, capture his license plate number and, second, follow him wherever he went—at a safe distance.

The twins had dressed for a chilly evening. They hid opposite the southwest corner of the house, behind a cluster of oaks, to ensure visibility of both the mansion's west-side backyard *and* the south-side coal chute.

Meanwhile, Roberta covered the facade of Number One, keeping her eyes peeled for the return of the flickering light. Based on its track record, no one expected the strange phenomena to occur until midnight. *Still, you never know.*

Roberta sat on her veranda, wrapped up in a comforter with a flask of hot chamomile tea at the ready beside her. "Oh, this is so much fun," she gushed when the five had met before the stakeout. "I'm delighted that you've included me in this mission."

Tom briskly downloaded a communication app that the mystery searchers often relied upon onto Roberta's cellphone. "Touch the screen here," he instructed, "and seconds later you'll be live with all four of us—sort of like a group walkie-talkie."

"Oh, my word. I've never heard of such a thing. Wonderful."

"You know what's remarkable?" Suzanne said to her brother as they settled in among the oaks. "Roberta's whole life changed the evening she met us at the birthday dinner. Now's she even talking to her best friend again."

"That's already made the entire case worthwhile," Tom said.

At that late hour, the traffic on hilly Pegasus Point Drive was close to nil. Kathy reached peak stakeout boredom almost instantly. Thirty minutes passed with only an occasional vehicle making its way in either direction. Then a white SUV appeared from the south.

"Check this guy out," Pete said. "He's driving awfully slow."

They watched the driver pull to the side of the road, cross the sidewalk, and park on the grassy area. *Right behind One Wainrich Manor.*

"It's a male," Kathy informed the group in an urgent whisper. "Just pulled over. He's getting out of his vehicle—and walking your way."

"Got him," Suzanne reported. "A shadow's crossing the back-yard, heading toward the mansion."

Beep-beep, beep-beep, beep-beep. Everyone had forgotten about the camera app. All four cellphones lit up.

"He's reached the back door," Tom said. "It looks like—*wow.* He's in."

"I think he used only one key . . ." Suzanne said.

"If he did," Roberta said, "he must've changed the locks."

"This is the guy who smashed and replaced the window," Tom said. "He'd handle the locks, no problem."

"Roberta," Kathy asked, "can you see a flashlight in there?"

"Nope. It's completely—*wait,* no, a beam of light just appeared. He's in the living room!"

Pete fired up the Mustang. "We're gonna get a picture of his license plate. Give us a shout if he exits the mansion." He backed out of the parking spot, hung a hard left onto Pegasus Point Drive, and pulled up behind the Jeep. "Go for it, Kathy!"

She jumped out and raced up to the vehicle, cellphone in hand. *Click. Click. Click.* Then she flipped around and leaped back into the front seat. Pete roared off, pulled a U-turn, and returned to their hiding spot.

"Here he comes!" Suzanne warned. *Beep-beep, beep-beep, beep-beep.*

"We got the license plate pic," Kathy said, sounding quite pleased with herself.

"Text it to Detective Ryan pronto," Tom said. "Tell him what's happening."

"Ten-four!" Pete couldn't believe how much fun this was.

"He's carrying something big," Suzanne said.

"And heavy," Tom said.

"Like what?" Roberta asked.

"It's hard to tell in the dark. It's shaped like a coffee table."

"Are you serious?" Roberta asked.

"Well . . . it's that shape."

A minute passed before Pete broke the silence. "He just popped out from the rocks, but he's not carrying anything. The guy's looking both ways . . ."

"He's making sure there're no cars coming," Kathy figured. "*Wait,* he turned around. Now—" She tapped the camera app icon on her phone and set the zoom to max.

"He's back," Pete cut in. "And he's loading something big into the Jeep."

"Does it look like a coffee table?" Roberta asked.

"Hard to say," Kathy said. "I got some closeups, pretty good shots of his face. He just slammed the back door. Now the guy's getting into the driver's seat and . . . yup, there he goes! *We'll follow him.*"

Pete gave the Jeep a thirty-second head start before pulling out onto Pegasus Point Drive.

Kathy's cellphone buzzed. She put the call on Speaker. "Hello."

A familiar voice with an East Texas drawl said, "I got the plate number. Is he still there?"

"Oh, hello, Detective Ryan! Nope, he just left. We're following him—it's one guy driving a newish white Jeep. He loaded up something from the mansion."

"He's a block in front of us!" Pete called out.

"Good chance he's heading home. The car's registered to James Arthur Bunker on Amicus Drive. Put that in your maps app. I'm heading that way now. Stay far enough back that he doesn't make you. Call me if you notice any change in direction—or if it looks like he's trying to shake you."

"Yes, sir," Pete replied.

Kathy reported the call to the others. The twins had already deserted Wainrich Manor and jumped into the Chevy.

"Roberta, I guess you can call it a night," Tom said. "Our 'ghost' is on his way home."

She laughed before disconnecting. "So I gather," she said. With the comms app live, she had been able to listen in on Detective Ryan's call. "I can't wait to tell Brenda!"

Amicus Drive was a twenty-minute drive away to the north-west section of the city. Without any visible sign of evasive driving, it seemed the Jeep's driver had no concern about being tailed.

Later, as the perp pulled into his driveway, an unmarked cruiser followed right behind him. Another vehicle came to a halt on the street out front. The Brunellis stopped, watching as a uniformed officer stepped out to provide backup. The detective briskly walked over to the driver's-side door. After a brief conversation, Mr. Bunker exited his Jeep and popped open the rear hatch.

The siblings witnessed Detective Ryan handcuffing the man and leading him to the cruiser.

Kathy kept the twins informed on the open comms app. "You guys were right. The guy swiped a coffee table from the mansion.

Detective Ryan just arrested him. He's heading off downtown in a police cruiser."

"A coffee table," Suzanne said. "Go figure. Why?"

"Who cares?" Pete declared, excited that they'd solved the mystery. He rubbed his hands in glee. "Another 'haunting' bites the dust!"

AFTER AN EXCITING AND EVENTFUL DAY, THE MYSTERY SEARCHERS hit the sack by 12:30 a.m. Suzanne was in a deep sleep when her cellphone, resting on her bedside table, buzzed only minutes later. It made quite a racket when she accidentally knocked it onto the floor. She picked it up and glanced at the screen, touching Answer.

"Roberta! Is everything okay?"

"Sorry to wake you at such an awful hour, dear, but I thought you should know."

"Know what?"

"The flickering light—it's back!"

9

TWO FOR ONE

On Sunday morning, the Jackson and Brunelli families attended church together before gathering at their favorite Mexican diner for brunch—a weekly tradition dating back many years. Tom had just bit into a cheese enchilada when a silent Incoming Call alert appeared on his cell phone.

"Hi, Detective Ryan. How are you doing?"

"I'm great, and I've got something for y'all down at the station. How about rounding up the others and meeting downtown?"

"We'll be there."

AN OFFICER LED THE FOURSOME TO A CONFERENCE ROOM WHERE Ryan sat in front of his notebook. He stood and greeted them. "Good morning. Take a seat. Anyone need water? Bottled waters are in that little fridge in the corner." He chuckled. "Y'all awake now?"

"We are," Suzanne replied. "Don't you ever sleep?"

"Every once in a while," the detective said with a shrug. "But police work keeps me rather busy. So today I have video to show you. I interviewed Mr. Bunker earlier, and he had quite a story to tell. This is from the interrogation room. I'll skip to the relevant parts."

The conference room door opened. Heidi Hoover stepped in, followed by the Chief. "Good afternoon," Ryan said, glancing up. "Grab a couple of seats. You'll find this quite interesting."

"Did Mr. Bunker admit to swiping the table?" Tom asked.

"Oh, yeah," he replied, "and lots more besides. Keep in mind what we're trying to do here. There are four objectives of an interrogation: to obtain valuable facts, to eliminate the innocent, to identify the guilty, and to gain a confession. Mr. Bunker cooperated and admitted his guilt. That made the process a lot easier. Let's jump to about . . . here."

A wall-mounted flat screen monitor lit up, displaying video of two men in a small interrogation room. The camera was positioned above them, pointing down at a forty-five-degree angle, with Detective Ryan seated with his back to the lens. A notebook rested on a small table before him, and he held a ballpoint pen at the ready. Opposite Ryan sat James Arthur Bunker, a short, heavyset man, middle-aged, with a pinched face, crow's feet around his eyes, and a pointed nose and chin. He had a big belly and needed a shave. And he looked nervous—very—as he sucked on coffee from a Styrofoam cup. He wore jeans and a short-sleeved flannel shirt. A light-weight jacket and wide-brimmed hat hung on the back of his chair.

"So," Detective Ryan began, "how long have you been looting One Wainrich Manor?"

"Six months," Mr. Bunker replied sullenly, "give or take."

"And you've sold everything on-line?

"Yup. The family packed the place with antiques. Can I smoke in here?"

"Sure. Go for it." The detective found an ashtray in a desk

drawer. He slid it across the table. As the mystery searchers well knew, officers always tried to make a suspect comfortable in an interrogation room. As the Chief often said, a suspect at ease is a suspect off guard. "Can you give me an idea of what you hauled out of there?"

Mr. Bunker struck a match and lit up his cigarette. His hands shook as he took a deep drag. "This is my first arrest, you know."

"Yes, sir. The court will take that into consideration."

"You're gonna find a list on my computer anyway, so . . . I grabbed everything I could lay my hands on. Whatever I could carry."

"Including furniture?"

"Like the coffee table? Yeah. And six chairs from the dining room. One at a time. A lot of the furniture is heavy. Too heavy. Like the dining room table, for example. It's massive. Or the six-foot high grandfather clock in the hallway. It's worth a fortune, but no way could I lift it. I swiped all the old English china and the silverware. An old television. Two ancient computers from the seventies—some people collect those old fossils. Seven pieces of art, including valuable oils. Odd and ends . . ."

"And it's all sold?"

"Yup. Every piece."

"How much total?"

Mr. Bunker thought for a moment. "Forty-five grand, I'd guess. Those oils were worth a small fortune."

Pete whistled softly as the mystery searchers glanced at one another with eyebrows raised.

On the monitor, Detective Ryan scribbled notes with his fountain pen. "Why did you choose the mansion?"

Mr. Bunker lifted his shoulders. "That place sat empty forever. After all this time, I didn't think I'd be hurting anyone. Even as a kid, I remember it being abandoned. So I broke in. It was easy picking."

"To gain access, you smashed a window?"

"Yup. Replaced it too, along with one lock on the back door. It had a second lock as well, but I disabled it."

"One thing that puzzles us," Ryan probed, "concerns the flickering light. What purpose did that serve?"

Mr. Bunker tilted his head. "Flickering light? I dunno what you're talking about."

That stopped Ryan. "You . . . never ran around the mansion with a light?"

"You're kidding, right? I'm there to rob the place, not to draw attention to myself. No way would I do that! Every time I got in there, it made me nervous. What would happen if someone spotted me? I wanted to get in and out. That's all."

The detective regrouped. "Early Saturday morning, right after midnight, you showed up in the mansion. You spent a minute or two inside before leaving empty-handed. Why?"

Mr. Bunker stared at him in surprise. "How—how did you know about that?"

"We had the house under surveillance."

The man rolled his head and looked up toward the ceiling. He took another drag on his cigarette. "Do you have any water?"

"Sure." Detective Ryan stepped over to a tiny corner fridge and dug out an ice-cold bottle of water. He twisted off the cap and handed it to Mr. Bunker. The man took a big gulp.

"I wasn't alone in there."

"What does that mean?"

A fearful look crossed his face. "I wasn't the only person in that house. Nor was it the first time that I felt another presence. A week earlier, a door slammed upstairs. Loud too. Something worse happened the other night, and it scared the heck out of me. I got out of there, quick-like."

"Worse? How?"

"It talked to me."

"'It'—*talked* to you?" Detective Ryan sat back in his chair.

"Yes."

His words reverberated around the conference room. Goose bumps ran up and down Kathy's spine. She frowned. It bugged her that her body was so much less skeptical than her brain.

"When you say '*it*' . . ." Ryan continued on the monitor.

"Well, I never saw it—or him, or whatever," Mr. Bunker said defensively. He slouched forward. "I just heard the words. Biggest shock of my life. I had just hoisted up that coffee table when a voice piped up."

"Saying what?"

"'Get out!'"

"'*Get out.*' That's it?"

"Uh-huh," he murmured. "Made my hair stand up. Not so much the words, although that was weird enough. But it came from somewhere behind me. I couldn't tell where, and it's as dark as coal in the mansion. But the way it spoke creeped me out."

"Like how?"

"Like . . . 'G-g-g-g-get o-o-out.' Stuttering, kind of. I took the advice, dropped the table, and got the heck out. Fast too."

"Male or female voice?"

"Male."

"Any kind of accent?"

"Nope."

Detective Ryan paused for a few seconds. "And yet you returned the next evening."

"That's a rare coffee table, a hundred years old, I'd guess. It's worth a ton. I figured, 'Why not?' One more time . . . get in and out, quick-like. I decided it'd be my last haul." He glanced across the table with a baleful expression. "Big mistake, huh?"

10

A SHOCKING SURPRISE

The monitor went dark. A collective silence enveloped the conference room before Detective Ryan cleared his throat. "Well, who's gonna start the discussion?"

"I will," Suzanne said, raising a hand. "Roberta called after midnight. The flickering light is back."

"Okay," Ryan said. "After Bunker's tale, that actually makes sense."

Kathy hesitated for a few seconds. "Mr. Bunker referred to the thing as 'it.' That bothered me."

"Means nothing," Tom figured out loud. "He never laid eyes on it."

"Even *you* are calling it an 'it' now!" Kathy wailed.

"Well, it's got a male voice, if that helps," Suzanne argued. She arched her eyebrows mysteriously. "Imagine two intruders sneaking around the mansion, neither of them knowing each other!"

"And one spying on the other," Tom noted.

Heidi's eyes flicked over to the detective. "Is this guy believable?"

"I think so. He has no reason to lie. Not now. And no previous record, either."

The Chief spoke up. "We have to assume there's someone else in there. Or *was* in there, anyway." He glanced over to Tom. "Is your camera still in place, and live?"

"Yes, sir."

"No other images after Mr. Bunker departed last night?"

"None."

The Chief cupped his nose with one hand. "So the second intruder could be in there, right now. Earlier, you mentioned something about keys."

"They're arriving tomorrow morning," Kathy replied. "Ten a.m. delivery, Fed-Ex."

"Good." Detective Ryan explained that the court would probably release Mr. Bunker, now languishing behind bars, because "he poses no threat of flight or violence in the community. He'll also be instructed by the judge not to go near One Wainrich Manor." For the time being, the thief was out of the picture.

"Okay," the Chief said, glancing toward his chief detective. "Let's conduct a floor-by-floor search in the morning."

"Meantime," Pete said, "we'll stake out the mansion tonight, just in case the light reappears."

"Oh, joy," Kathy murmured.

LATER THAT DAY, RIGHT BEFORE 3:00 P.M., THE CAMERA APP uploaded more images. A man had circled around to the back of Number One. He wore jeans, boots, and a warm jacket. Huge sunglasses protected his eyes from the blinding glare of the sun reflecting off the remaining patches of snow. He carried a big broom in one hand.

"Gotta be Henry Travers," Suzanne deduced. "He's the maintenance guy Dorothy mentioned. Looks like he's gonna sweep the snow off the veranda."

"That makes sense," Tom said. "I wonder if Mr. Travers has seen any sign of intruders?"

"I dunno. Let's call Roberta. We should talk with him."

Roberta answered on the first ring. "Henry is at Number One right now. I'll ask him to stay until you get here."

Fifteen minutes later, the mystery searchers pulled into the cul-de-sac and came to a stop in Roberta's driveway. Mr. Travers—a clean-shaven man, about five foot seven, with a medium build—stepped out from her house and onto the veranda.

After introductions and a bit of chitchat, Tom asked, "How long have you worked for the homeowners on Wainrich Manor?"

"Oh, man," Mr. Travers replied, tilting his head in thought. "I'm guessing twenty years."

"So you're familiar with all three houses and their grounds," Kathy said.

"Like the back of my hand," he replied.

"Have you noticed anything unusual happening here in the last month?" Suzanne asked.

"Nothing much happens out here," Mr. Travers said. "No real traffic and few pedestrians on the cul-de-sac, of course. But I did notice an odd uptick in activity about a week ago."

That piqued their interest. "Like what, sir?" Pete asked.

"Well, I had swept snow from Number One's veranda," he replied. "We try to keep the wood dry so it doesn't rot away any more than it has. I was up there"—he raised a shoulder toward the mansion—"on the right side of the veranda. See those living room curtains?"

The mystery searchers craned their necks. "Uh-huh," Kathy replied.

"They moved."

The four chorused, "They moved?"

"Yup. Not much—just a little. At first, I figured I was seeing things, but it seemed real. I shook my head and forgot about it, but after what Mrs. Robertson just told me . . . well, anything's possible."

"No footprints in the snow?" Suzanne asked.

"Well, yes, as a matter of fact." He looked away for a bit. "A few days ago, I spotted footprints coming and going from the back door. But the mansion's locked up tight, so I didn't worry about it. People often come by to gawk at the mansion. In fact, they take *selfies* in front of it. Some even trespass, walk across the grounds. Harmless. And although we've had snow a few times over the last week, we had ten days prior without a snowfall. But . . . yeah. Not too unusual, I'd say."

"Brunellis' turn for a stakeout," Suzanne said to her best friend as the foursome headed back to their cars a few minutes later.

"I think you should arrive at Wainrich Manor by eleven tonight," Tom said. "Just in case."

"Why so early?" Kathy objected. "The intruder makes his run at midnight. All we'll do is freeze to death while we wait for—well, whatever."

"Hey," Pete insisted, "we gotta be ready for anything . . ."

THAT WAS THE NIGHT WHEN A SERIES OF UNIMAGINABLE EVENTS changed everything. First, "it" materialized again on the third floor. The siblings watched, mesmerized, as it journeyed down, pausing on the second floor, skipping the first, and heading into the basement, opening and closing the hatch. And then Pete rushed over and twisted the hatch door open. *And then they were in!*

That awful basement smell . . . and rats! *Gross.*

And those stairs! Without realizing it, the siblings traveled up opposite sets leading to the landing on the first floor. Just as they reached the top, a clock—it had to be huge—chimed away from somewhere within the mansion, deep and jarring. *Bong, bong, bong, bong* . . . all the way to midnight.

What? How? Why?

Kathy grasped the doorknob and turned it ever so slowly. She cracked the door open a couple of inches. It creaked. She angled her neck and peered through the narrow opening. Too dark to see a thing. She opened it wider, taking one step in.

Something moved.

Whack! The bristles of a broom landed with full force on Kathy's head. *"Pete!"* she shrieked, raising one arm to protect herself. Her other hand grasped the door frame, hanging on for dear life, as she tried her best not to fall backward into that stinky, rat-infested basement.

Someone grunted before hammering Kathy twice more.

Whack! Whack!

"Stop it!" Kathy yelled, punching forward blindly. *"Pete!"*

"What are you doing here?" a woman's voice screamed. "Why are you frightening people?"

A second later, Pete grabbed the broom with one hand and locked Kathy's assailant around her waist with his other arm. "Leave her alone!" he demanded in a tone that brooked no argument.

"Who are you?" the woman yelled, her voice shaky as she struggled in Pete's grip.

"Never mind who *we* are," Pete said, his teeth clenched. *"Who are you?"*

Kathy, trying to calm her beating heart, found her cellphone and tapped the flashlight icon with a trembling finger. She aimed the beam of light toward the pair, revealing a small woman with frightened eyes, silver hair, and high cheekbones.

It took a second to register before Kathy blurted, "Oh, my gosh. Hello, Dorothy."

11

THE SEARCH

"How did you recognize me?" Dorothy Wainrich demanded, crossing her arms. Two cellphone flashlights illuminated the trio harshly, casting eerie shadows on the vast walls of the cold, dark kitchen.

It soon dawned on the Brunellis that Dorothy was the opposite of her childhood friend. *Curt, businesslike, borderline rude,* Pete thought.

"Roberta has a treasured picture," Kathy replied quickly, "of the two of you. Your first day at Prescott High. It's sitting atop the fireplace in her living room. You've got those high cheekbones."

"Pfffft," Dorothy groused. "That woman was sentimental sixty years ago. Nothing's changed." She scowled across the table at the siblings. "Imagine sneaking around my house at midnight. You're darn lucky I didn't have a pistol handy."

"We're here because Roberta asked us for help," Pete said. "You've got a severe case of uninvited intruders."

"You're a pretty insolent young man," Dorothy shot back at him. "Roberta doesn't own this house. I do."

Headlights swept into the house as a car turned into the cul-de-sac. "That'll be Tom and Suzanne," Kathy said. "They're the other half of our mystery team. Could you open up the doors for them?"

"Oh, great," Dorothy grumbled, "more uninvited visitors." The three stepped down the long hallway to the front door. On the way, Pete touched his sister's shoulder and pointed toward an enormous grandfather clock ticking away. Dorothy pulled out a set of keys from her pocket and released two locks before swinging the double doors wide open. The siblings walked out onto the veranda, waving as the twins rushed forward before freezing in their tracks, surprised to see a stranger with their friends.

"Suzanne and Tom, say hello to Dorothy Wainrich Chase."

Somewhere upstairs, a door squeaked on its hinges.

For the first time, Dorothy looked uneasy. "We're not alone." She spun around. "Grab my suitcase, young man," she said to Pete, pointing to a rollaboard against the wall in the hallway. "We're outta here." It wasn't a request. It was an order.

MINUTES LATER, THE MYSTERY SEARCHERS AND DOROTHY SAT crowded around Roberta's kitchen table as a still sleepy Roberta, dressed in an elegant housecoat, made tea for everyone.

Tom asked, "What time did you arrive, Dorothy?"

"I took an Uber from the airport after a very uncomfortable flight. I got here just before eleven p.m."

"You beat us by a few minutes," Pete said.

"It's been sixty years since you visited the mansion," Suzanne said, trying to draw Dorothy out. "What were your first impressions?"

She looked away for a moment. "Not that it matters, but the place is exactly the way I remember it. Even when I walked in, the grandfather clock ticked away." Her eyes narrowed as they circled the table. "Did you wind it up?"

"No, of course not!" Kathy said.

The twins were still trying to understand what they had missed. "So you spotted the flickering light upstairs," Tom said, his eyes resting on their best friends. "It made its way into the basement. Then you forced open the hatch, slipped down and made your way upstairs. Where did the light go?"

"No clue," Pete replied. "It just vanished. Looked to me as if it exited through the hatch."

"That's not how I saw it," Kathy said. "The hatch lifted and lowered, *then* the light went out. Whoever was carrying it around is obviously still inside the mansion . . . And guess what? That basement is infested with rats."

Dorothy raised her feet off the floor. "Rats? You gotta be kidding. *I hate rats.*"

Pete couldn't help himself. "Well, after sixty years. . ."

"Dorothy," Suzanne asked, "did *you* see the flickering light?"

"I did not," she answered. "But I heard it."

"You heard the light?" Suzanne asked.

"I heard whoever was moving around with it. Someone walked down the front stairs from the second floor. I grabbed the broom and hid in the kitchen, trying not to breathe too hard. If the intruder came anywhere near me, I had an unpleasant surprise waiting. The footsteps continued down into the basement."

"That must be when we watched as the hatch opened and closed," Pete said.

"It got quiet for three or four minutes," Dorothy added, "before I heard steps coming up the stairs . . . and then voices. That's when you appeared," she said, pointing to Kathy. "And I whacked you with the broom."

"You certainly did," Kathy said. "That was a surprise."

"Uh-huh. For me too."

"You'll stay here safely with me tonight," Roberta said to her old friend as she poured the steaming tea, "and as long as you need to."

Kathy looked around the table. "I say we call it a night."

———

FIRST THING ON MONDAY AFTERNOON, A SMALL ARMY DESCENDED upon One Wainrich Manor. The mystery searchers parked in Roberta's driveway and walked over, accompanied by Roberta and Dorothy.

Roberta treated the episode like a day at camp, full of fun and adventure. Dorothy appeared ready for battle.

"When will you learn to enjoy life?" Roberta challenged her friend. "There's a mysterious entity roaming around your family home. Let's go say hello!"

"You never grew up, did you?" Dorothy cracked back.

In rapid succession, Heidi Hoover, Detective Joe Ryan, and the Chief pulled into the cul-de-sac and parked. Introductions followed. Dorothy frowned the whole time.

"She's still quite disagreeable today," Kathy noted.

"She'll warm up," Suzanne felt sure. "It'll just take time."

Pete grunted. "Good luck with that."

Dorothy unlocked the two side-by-side front doors and opened them wide. Detective Ryan gathered everyone around inside.

"The Chief and I will lead," he explained. "We'll start off on the third floor and work our way down. If we find nothing there, we'll split into two groups as we go from floor to floor. One group will descend along the west stairs at the back of the house, the other the east stairs at the front. We'll meet again on each floor. Our goal is to search each floor before progressing to the basement."

"We're assuming," the Chief said, "that the intruder is some-where in the house. I'm asking everyone to follow behind Detective Ryan and myself. Don't get ahead of us, no matter what. Questions?"

Silence.

"All right. Let's go," the detective said. "Dorothy, it would be helpful if you could provide commentary on each floor."

Everyone made their way briskly up to the third floor.

"There are three bedrooms here," Dorothy explained. "I was only six when we moved into the mansion. My bedroom was to the right, and my brother Bill's to the left. My parents reserved the third bedroom for visiting friends and cousins. We all shared one bathroom at the end of the hall."

It amazed the group to see everything still in place, sixty years later—furniture, artworks on the walls, clothes, books, bedding, carpets, toothbrushes, toothpaste. *All still there.* No sign that anyone had been there in decades. Bunker appeared not to have stolen anything from the top floor.

On the second floor, there were two large bedrooms, each with its own bathroom. "Mom slept in this one," Dorothy explained. "My grandparents had the one at the end of the hall."

They made their way to Rupert and Barbara Wainrich's bedroom.

"Oh, my gosh," Dorothy said as she walked in. "Someone's pulled the bedsheets back—and slept here, recently too."

Heidi grabbed a quick shot of the bed and the crowd of people around it.

In the ground-floor dining room, a giant china cabinet sat empty, its doors splayed wide open. An old, ornate dining table squatted in the center of the room, without chairs.

In the adjacent living room, Dorothy noted that two antique side chairs and a coffee table that she remembered clearly had also all vanished. She pointed out the impressions their feet had left, sunk deep into the dusty Oriental carpet—all evidence of Bunker's intrusions.

She glared at the Chief. "I hope you throw the book at him," she growled ominously.

Nothing else showed the recent presence of a human being. Not in the kitchen, library, butler's pantry, bathrooms, or hallways. The basement turned up empty as well.

"Maybe it *is* a ghost," Pete said, just to bug his sister.

She shot him a certain look. "Ghosts don't sleep in beds."

The group gathered in a circle in the living room. "I don't think there's any sign of an intruder hiding anywhere in the home right now," Detective Ryan declared. "Does anyone disagree?"

Silenced reigned until Roberta's small voice spoke up. "I do."

That surprised Dorothy. "You disagree? You think a stranger is in the house?"

"Yes, for sure."

"Why?" the Chief asked.

"I don't know what it is, sir," she replied. "But someone keeps appearing at will. Someone is just here—*whenever they want to be.* How do we explain that?"

12

A CHALLENGE

That night, the entire group rendezvoused again. They began arriving at Wainrich Manor just after 11:30 p.m. Fifteen minutes later, everyone sat in folding chairs in front of Number Two.

Roberta had the boys drag out a freestanding potbellied wood-fired stove from the garage. It threw off a good amount of heat, taking the chill off the late-night air. They all enjoyed an excellent view of the mansion's facade.

She also brought out flasks of hot chocolate and served the group—including Dorothy, who had parked herself in the center of the activity. The girls found the scene amusing. "Roberta's throwing a party," Kathy whispered, "and Dorothy's enjoying herself. A first!"

A few of the visitors—the twins, Dorothy, Heidi, Detective Ryan, and the Chief—had never seen the flickering light. An air of anticipation rippled through the group as they all chatted amicably.

For Heidi, the story looked promising. "Front-page stuff, if it's real." She brought along a Nikon digital camera with a super-tele-photo lens. "Does the intruder show up every night?"

"Well, no," Roberta answered. "Three out of four nights so far. I wondered if the crowd might scare off our uninvited guest."

"I'd like to go over and smack him one," Dorothy muttered.

"Yes, ma'am, I believe you would," Detective Ryan observed. By now, everyone had come to know her. "But that's not a good idea."

"Why not? It's my house."

"Uh-huh, I understand that. But we don't have the faintest clue who we're dealing with. Let's figure things out first. He might not even show tonight."

"You spoke too soon," the Chief said, sitting upright in his folding chair.

Kathy blanched. "Our old friend is back."

"What the heck is it?" Heidi said, as the soft *click-click* of her Nikon resonated in the hushed night.

"You got me," the Chief replied.

Detective Ryan stared intently. "He's on the second floor."

"Will he travel up or down?" Heidi asked.

"Yes," Pete cracked.

Heidi jumped out of her chair and tore off into the night, leading the crowd toward Number One. "Where's the hatch?" she called out.

"To the left!" Roberta shouted.

A minute or two later, everyone had circled around the glass relic. "Here it comes," Dorothy growled. The glow drew closer, a soft blur under the pitted glass, and seemed to drift halfway up the chute's stairs.

Heidi switched her camera from still to video mode.

"Stand back," Kathy whispered. "Last time it opened the hatch." But whoever—or whatever—it never reached the top of the steps. Instead, the light paused before backing off and fading away to nothing.

Suzanne realized she had been holding her breath. "Well, that was interesting."

"Does this open?" Detective Ryan muttered. He reached down and pulled up on the metal handle. He yanked a second time. "It's locked."

"You gotta pull hard," Pete offered. He bent down and grabbed the handle with both hands. He put his back into it. "What the heck . . . it won't even budge."

"You want in? Follow me," Dorothy ordered. She led the way over to the front and unlocked both doors. "Have at it."

With Detective Ryan and the Chief leading, Heidi and the mystery searchers followed close behind. The two older ladies brought up the rear. Police flashlights and cellphone beams scanned the interior as the team surged down into the basement.

Nothing but a strange odor. *Kerosene*, Tom thought.

The officers split up, taking the two sets of stairs and racing to the third floor.

No sign of anyone . . . or anything. Nor was there any indication of recent activity on the second floor. Or on the first. *Nada.*

The camera app on the mystery searchers' cellphones didn't ping. No one had escaped through the back door.

The team regrouped, forming a circle in the living room. Pete shrugged. "I don't get it."

"Lights don't move by themselves," the Chief declared. "Someone's hiding in here."

"I told you, sir," Roberta reminded him.

The Chief couldn't help but smile. "Yes, you did."

Heidi slipped away to wander around the first floor, capturing images. As she stepped into the dining room, she shot a close-up of the empty china cabinet. The massive dining room table caught her attention too. Her built-in electronic flash burst every few seconds.

A minute later, as Heidi showed the girls the pictures, Suzanne spotted something. "Hey, check this out," she called out. A thick layer of dust, unperturbed for decades, had coated the dining room table. Nothing had stood out to the naked eye with the flashlight beams bouncing around, but the raking light of Heidi's flash had revealed a message.

Suzanne's tone of voice brought everyone crowding into the room.

"What is it?" Detective Ryan asked.

"Special delivery for you," Suzanne quipped. "Written in the dust on the dining table. Check out Heidi's LCD display."

The officers leaned closer.

"'Get out!'" the Chief read the words out loud.

"'*Get out?*'" Roberta asked.

"Uh-huh," Heidi confirmed. "It's hard to read. But look—" She turned her cellphone flashlight on and pointed it at the table from a shallow angle. "You can make out the handwritten letters."

Detective Ryan bent lower, squinting as he too projected a light beam from his cell and slowly circled the immense dining table. "Well, how about that? In block letters: 'Get out!'"

"I have a question," Heidi asked no one in particular.

"Like what?" Pete asked.

"Is this individual friend or foe?"

No answer, at first.

"Who knows," Suzanne said finally. "One thing's for sure. We're dealing with real flesh and blood—even if we can't find him. Or her. Yet."

At breakfast on Tuesday morning, the twins harangued their father in a search for ideas.

"C'mon, Dad," Suzanne said. "Who left that message? And why? Was it intended for us?"

"Could be." The Chief took a sip of coffee.

"So, what can we do? I mean, we have to figure this out."

"Yes, you do."

"Any ideas?" Tom urged.

"You're the high-tech guy," the Chief said, squinting over to Tom with one eye shut. "Can't you use technology to track this intruder?"

"Yeah," Tom replied, "I've been thinking about it. I mean, this person must need food. Eventually, they're gonna be forced to leave the mansion to pick up groceries. If he slips out back, *bang*, the camera will capture him."

Suzanne agreed. "And if he escapes out front, Roberta would spot him."

"That's a long shot," the Chief argued. "She isn't *always* at a window or out on her veranda."

"Well . . . how about . . ." Inspiration struck. "An underground tunnel?" Suzanne asked.

"To where?" Tom asked. "There's nothing around except two other houses."

The Chief grinned, finished his coffee with a last gulp, and stood up. "Keep thinking outside the box."

13

A HIGH-TECH SOLUTION

"Okay," Kathy prompted. "Tell us your idea."

The mystery searchers had gathered an hour later to talk strategy. Pete sprawled on the Jackson's living room floor, munching an apple. The girls sat on the couch while Tom took over an easy chair.

"Well, I've got a couple thoughts," Tom said.

Pete yawned. "Whatever, bro. Share."

"The individual wandering around inside the mansion carries an old-fashioned lantern."

"Meaning?" Suzanne asked.

"Meaning nothing. That's what he or she is *carrying*. It's oil-based, with a wick, and it flickers. They'd have been common back in Rupert Wainrich's parents' day. Some people still keep them on hand for power outages."

"Or it could be a replica of a lantern," Kathy said, "like the flameless lanterns and candles used for fire safety reasons in theater."

Pete shook his head. "I doubt it. Remember that kerosene odor?"

"True," Kathy conceded. "That light has all the earmarks of an actual flame."

Pete finished the apple, wiping his mouth with the back of his hand. "What's this guy surviving on? I mean, everybody's gotta eat, right?"

His sister shot him the look. "Is that all you think about?"

"Good point," Tom said. "The intruder might've checked in with a big sack of food."

"Which brings up an interesting question," Suzanne said. "We know how Bunker gained access. How did this other intruder get in?"

"No clue at this stage of the game," Tom replied.

Pete asked, "So how are we gonna nail him?"

Tom leaned forward. "Well, I've been thinking."

"Always dangerous," his sister teased.

"Last year," Tom continued, "the technology club played with thermal radiation detection."

"Never heard of it," said Kathy. "What's it used for?"

"Security, mostly," Tom replied, "for detecting the presence of people."

"*Game on!*" Pete exclaimed. "Just what the doctor ordered. How's it work?"

"Imagine a sensor attached to an integrated circuit," Tom continued, "inside a small, flat box. Wireless, powered by long-lasting miniature batteries. We hide the device in the corner of a room, up high. It projects an invisible floor grid of squares that covers almost the entire space."

"A grid invisible to the human eye," Suzanne clarified, "with two-foot squares."

Tom nodded. "Right. As a person or an animal walks across the grid, the sensor detects their presence by measuring a transfer of heat from square to square."

"Wait a sec," Pete said. "How big is this sensor?"

"Small," Suzanne replied. "The size of a credit card, but a quarter-inch thick."

"Wouldn't our intruder spot it?" Kathy asked.

"Good question," Tom replied. "I considered that, and sure, anything's possible. But the basement and first-floor ceilings are high. Not an issue in my mind—easy to hide the sensors. The second and third floors both have lower ceilings. Somehow, we'll have to disguise those two sensors."

"We'd install one on each floor?"

"Uh-huh. The club's got four of them, which is great. It's the only way to track the intruder in a house that size."

"It's awesome," Suzanne said. "Tom showed us how it works last year. It even impressed Dad. As a person walks across the invisible electronic grid, a sensor uploads a thermal image tracking their movement to the Cloud."

"You can't really *see* the person," Tom explained. "What you get is a pixilated, rainbow-colored silhouette. Of him, or her, or multiple people, but the image is clear enough that you can follow their movements. It'll show us where someone is coming from—or going."

"Why not just move the camera indoors?" Kathy asked.

"Too difficult to hide," Tom said, "plus, we only have one camera. We can borrow four thermal detectors."

"And," Suzanne mentioned, "they can download the images to our cellphones in real time, and the app always indicates which sensors are being triggered."

"How cool is that!" Kathy exclaimed.

"Uh-huh. Check it out." Tom pulled out his cell and found a video he had saved months earlier. Pete jumped to his feet as the girls gathered around. A blobby, roughly pixilated shape of a person, red and orange and yellow in the warm torso and head area, green and blue at the cooler extremities, moved across an outlined grid over the screen, constantly shifting in contour.

Pete couldn't believe it. "Love it! What are we waiting for?"

A thought crossed Suzanne's mind. "Disguising the sensors isn't a problem. The entire interior of the mansion is a soft off-white color. Kathy and I'll drive over there now. We'll take paint chips and match the color."

"Perfect," Kathy said. "Then we'll create a cardboard cover for the sensors—spray-painted to match—with only the aperture peeking out. We'll hide the finished product in the stairwell corners using double-sided gel tape."

Suzanne grabbed her keys. "Let's go."

While the girls headed over to Wainrich Manor, Tom and Pete made their way back to Ray's for a hardware pickup.

"No problem," Ray said when Tom called him from the Chevy. "You still need the camera?"

"We do," Tom replied. "Just for a few more days. Don't worry. It's well protected."

With four sensor devices in hand, the mystery searchers laid out their implementation plan. So far, the intruder had appeared on the second or third floors before beginning his or her journey. And the individual always appeared to traverse the front stairwell—never the back. So it made sense to place the sensors in the front stairwell, pointing back toward the main hallway on each of the top three floors, and near the front stairs targeting the coal chute hatch in the basement.

A COUPLE OF HOURS SLIPPED BY BEFORE THE FOURSOME CONVERGED on Number Two.

"Come on in," Roberta greeted them. Pete tried his best to avoid her embrace, but she managed to hug each of them.

Suzanne smiled and hugged her back. "We're doing fine,

Roberta. Our little technology initiative is ready, and we thought we'd give you a preview."

"Dorothy's in the kitchen. Would you like some tea or coffee?"

The group gathered around the kitchen table. When Tom played the video of the thermal footage on his cellphone, the two women got it instantly.

Even Dorothy seemed impressed. "This might show us where the intruder is hiding."

"That's the idea," Tom said. "We're hopeful it'll work." He had installed the thermal radiation software on his laptop the previous school year, as well as an app on his cellphone that could stream the footage in real time. The installation of the sensors came next.

The foursome made their way over to Number One and unlocked the front door. Pete found a rickety wooden ladder in the basement. An hour passed as the foursome planted a sensor on each floor. They worked as a unit, as quietly as possible, concerned that the intruder might make a surprise appearance. After installing each device, they ran a test and watched as the streaming video download appeared on Tom's cellphone.

"The image is pretty clear," Kathy whispered, "in its rainbow, pixilated way. What's it look like at night?"

"Identical," Tom replied quietly. "The sensors detect heat, not light. If he shows, we'll see him."

Before they installed the final sensor, Pete excused himself. He slipped outside and made his way to the south side of the house to stand over the multi-sided glass hatch. Earlier, Suzanne had wondered out loud how the intruder had gained access to the mansion. Pete didn't have an answer, but a thought had occurred to him.

Two days before, after a great deal of effort, he had yanked the hatch open only to hear it lock—or jam—again as he lowered it from the inside. Yet the previous night, neither Detective Ryan nor Pete could budge it from outside. *Why?*

Pete reached down and yanked hard. Nothing. He tried to remember exactly what he had done previously. He squatted down and lifted with a hard push to the right. Nada. Then he tried again, this time pulling hard to the left. *It clicked open!* He raised the hatch, slipped under it, and stepped down onto the old wooden steps. He flipped around and faced the opposite direction, allowing the hatch to close above him. *Click.* He pushed up, hard. It wouldn't budge. Then he pushed again, this time angling to his right. *It opened again.*

"That explains it," he murmured.

14

AN IDEA

After completing the installation, the foursome stopped back at Number Two.

"We'll return tonight after eleven o'clock," Suzanne said. "Everything's ready."

"Wonderful," Roberta said.

Something had occurred to Kathy. *It's probably nothing,* she thought. *Still.* "Dorothy, I have a question for you. The last year you lived here, Roberta mentioned that you spent the summer in New Hampshire."

"That's correct," she replied, looking away for a few seconds. "Mom, my brother, and me. The entire summer, really, except for the last two weeks. We stayed with my grandparents on my father's side."

"Was that the only time?"

"No, we traveled to New Hampshire *every* summer, but only for a week or two. That year we spent over two months there. My grandparents lived on the coast, within walking distance of the ocean. We loved visiting them—and the ocean—but I think we wore "Got it," Kathy said. "Your family left because of construction, right?"

Dorothy looked at her. "Uh-huh. It was kind of sudden. One day, Mom announced that Granddad wanted to renovate the mansion. Paint, new cupboards in this kitchen"—she pointed around the room—"the bathrooms . . . just about the entire house. That's when he added those three bedrooms downstairs. Back then, we had company all the time. So Mom said, 'Fine, we're leaving,' and off we went. Took four days to drive there."

"And when you returned, they had completed the renovation work?"

"Yes. It felt like walking into a new home. I remember Mom being overjoyed about how the house looked."

The mystery searchers chatted all the way back to the Jacksons'.

"Another fun night, this time with fireworks," Pete quipped. He rubbed his hands together in anticipation.

Suzanne agreed. "We'll be out front and watching on our cells as well."

"I'll set up links for everyone," Tom said.

"Where did you disappear to?" Kathy asked her brother.

"I checked out the hatch over the coal chute. It's the only way the intruder could access the mansion. And I figured it out. From outside, you yank the hatch hard and to the left—it pops open every time. From inside, hard and to the right."

"Good for you, bro!" Tom exclaimed.

"Oh, wow," Suzanne said. "Short of breaking a window, that makes total sense."

"I've got something too," Kathy said. "It's just an idea, but . . ."

"Tell us," Suzanne urged.

"Well . . ." She hesitated. "We all agree an intruder's hiding in there. *But where?* We've turned the place upside down. Not even a hint, right?"

"Right," the other three chorused.

"So there *must be* a secret hiding place. Underground, but not necessarily a tunnel. So well hidden that we don't have a clue where it is. And neither does Dorothy."

"Why *wouldn't* Dorothy know?" Suzanne asked.

"Because she wasn't there when they built it!" Kathy exclaimed. "I think Mr. Wainrich had it installed during the summer when her family vacationed in New Hampshire."

Silence descended for a few seconds before Tom spoke up. "Whoa, Kathy. You might be on to something. I wonder if the city required construction permits back then?"

"Sure they would."

"Dynamite!" Pete exclaimed. "How do we find out?"

"Remember Bill Holden?" Suzanne asked. "The city's chief engineer? We worked with him on the case of the ghost in the county courthouse. If the permit records still exist, he can help us find them."

"I have his direct number," Tom said, reaching for his cellphone.

AT FOUR O'CLOCK THAT AFTERNOON, THE MYSTERY SEARCHERS walked into Bill Holden's City Hall office. Bill was a tall man with a square jaw and closely cropped hair, and a friendly, calm demeanor. The foursome had worked well with him.

"Great to see you all," he said. He stood and shook hands with each of them. "Grab a seat. I haven't talked to you since the county courthouse case. Meanwhile, you guys have made quite the name for yourselves. I've been following your exploits in *The Daily Pilot.* How can I help?"

Suzanne plunged in. "Funny you should mention the courthouse, Bill. We're working on another strange one." The others joined in as the city engineer sat back, taking in every word. The foursome explained how it had all begun: the random meeting with Roberta Robertson at the Chief's birthday party, and the strange flickering light that made regular midnight runs through One Wainrich Manor. About Brenda and her family fleeing Number Three, and the capture of Bunker, the man who had looted the mansion. And Dorothy's unexpected return.

"Bunker smashed a window to get in," Pete explained. "But we think the midnight intruder gained access through an old, multi-sided glass hatch that covers the coal chute. It'll open if you know how to do it."

"How would the intruder know?" Bill asked.

"Good question," Tom replied. "Maybe they just kept trying, the way I did. There are no answers. Nor do we have a clue who this person is. Or why they're hiding."

"But we've got a hunch," Suzanne continued, "about the hiding place itself."

Since it was her idea, Kathy explained about Dorothy's summer absence sixty years earlier. "Only then could they add a room without her knowledge. Our question is, would permits be required back in the day? And would they still exist?"

Bill got to his feet. "Follow me." They trekked through a maze of corridors to an underground passageway, and through a door marked Records. "Hello, Mildred."

A much older woman, tiny, with short, grey hair and glasses, appeared behind a counter. "Hi, Bill. What brings you down here?"

"These are friends of mine. You've read about Prescott's own mystery searchers, right?" He introduced the four.

"Oh, sure," she replied in surprise. "You guys worked on the tunnel case on Whiskey Row, didn't you? I remember that so well."

"Yes, ma'am," Suzanne replied. "That was such an intriguing

mystery. Now we're searching for information on an abandoned mansion, and we need to see permits issued, sixty years ago last summer."

"Oh, my," Mildred replied. "That's a very long time ago. Do you have the address?"

15

PIXILATED IMAGES

W hat appeared to be endless shelves ten feet high held thousands of boxes and *millions* of documents.

The searchers had a rough date to work with. "I'd guess April or May that year, based on a summer construction," Kathy said. And, of course, the address: One Wainrich Manor.

Mildred led the way, walking between a row of shelves to a concrete wall many yards farther along before hanging a left turn. She counted out the years row by row before coming to a sudden halt. "Here's where you can start. If a permit exists, it'll be in this area. Good luck." She turned and walked away.

Bill jumped into the search with the foursome, seeming to enjoy himself immensely. They recalled how much he liked mysteries. He grabbed a rolling ladder and pulled it all the way down the aisle. "I'll yank the boxes from the top and hand them down. Ready?"

An hour later, they struck pay dirt—that's what Pete called it, which caused Kathy to giggle. A dusty cardboard box that had large, handwritten notations on two opposite sides in faded ink: One Wainrich Manor. Tom brushed away cobwebs as multiple hands removed dozens of documents and spread them across the concrete floor.

"Most of these are property tax docs," Bill noted.

"Water meter readings too," Pete read out loud.

"Here's a construction permit, but it's the wrong date," Kathy said, disappointed.

"Serious?" Tom asked. "For what, and when?"

"Widening the veranda a decade earlier."

"Well, we gotta be close," Bill said.

Five minutes later, Suzanne shouted, "Eureka!"

"Whatcha got?" Pete asked.

"What we've been searching for." She laid it out on the floor, smoothing out brittle, yellowed documents faded by time, and spreading them apart.

"Well, well." Bill checked the date. "Yup, this is it! No-one's looked at this in a very long while."

Everyone gathered around and fell to their knees, eagerly scanning the documents. A dated cover page with the Wainriches' name and address—stamped *City Of Prescott, Residential Construction Permits*—covered six permit sheets, each with a handwritten item that detailed a specific project. The first page covered a "Two-foot kitchen extension, including new cupboards, flooring, electrical, etc. Total price—$3,200.00" Page two read: "Buildout of three 8'x10' bedrooms in the basement. Total price—$5,345.00."

"You'd never get away with this today," Bill pointed out. "We require measured instructions, blueprints, and much more detail."

"A lot more dough too," Pete said.

But it was the last page that caught everyone's attention.

"Whoo-hoo, Kathy!" exclaimed Suzanne. "You were right. Check it out."

It read: "Construction of an underground shelter: 12'x12'x8', requiring extensive excavation, water, new walls, and flooring. Total price: $12,500.00."

High-fives circled the aisle. *"Good job!"* Pete all but shouted at his sister.

"We used to call them doomsday shelters," Bill said, chuckling. "Preparing for the worst, which never came."

Kathy smiled, enjoying the accolades. "But we still have a big problem, don't we?"

That stopped Pete. "What do you mean? Like what?"

"Like it doesn't show *where* the underground shelter is," Tom replied. "And we sure never spotted it when we surveyed the basement."

Pete shrugged. "So what? We'll search again. And if that fails, your pixel thing will come in real handy."

Tom couldn't help chuckling. "It's not a pixel thing. It's a thermal radiation detector."

"Yeah, whatever," Pete said. "Now we've loaded the bases. Let's go hit a home run."

The foursome thanked Bill and Mildred before heading out.

A disagreement soon broke out in the car. Pete wanted to rush over to Number One and begin searching for the doomsday shelter. But he couldn't get any takers.

"Why not?" he demanded.

"Because we might frighten the intruder away," Suzanne argued, "and who knows what would happen next? Plus, the shelter is certainly well hidden. Let's let the thermal imaging show us the way—tonight. Then investigate in person by daylight tomorrow."

"Fine," Pete said, surrendering. "A doomsday shelter—I like it. It's got a certain ring to it."

THE PARTY BEGAN AT ELEVEN O'CLOCK THAT EVENING AT ROBERTA'S home. At least, that's what Pete called it.

Heidi joined them a few minutes later, about the same time as Detective Ryan.

"Where's your father?" Roberta asked the twins.

"Some kind of emergency at the station," Tom replied.

First things first. They brought copies of the permits over to show Detective Ryan. Heidi and the two older ladies checked them over as well. The revelation surprised Dorothy but didn't shock her.

"My grandfather was what you might call a 'prepper' today," she explained. "He always stocked water, canned goods, toilet paper, you name it. 'The day will come when we'll run out of everything,' he often said. And he prepared for it. "This"—she pointed to the permits—"is classic Grandpa."

"Well, it certainly isn't your grandfather hiding down there," Roberta declared. "He'd be well over a hundred years old by now."

"You had no clue of the bunker's existence?" Pete asked Dorothy.

"None. You've been in the basement. Did you see any evidence?"

The mystery searchers glanced at one another. "Nope," Kathy said.

"Me neither," Dorothy said.

"If your grandfather was so open about his 'prepper' obsession," Suzanne asked, "why did he keep the shelter a secret?"

"Your guess is as good as mine."

"It's a mystery," Detective Ryan said. "When we solve it, it'll look simple enough."

Once again, Roberta had the boys drag out the potbellied stove and place it in the front yard to ward off the frigid late-night air. The girls dragged out folding chairs from Roberta's basement and placed them close to the heat.

The two ladies brought out flasks of hot chocolate and cookies. Heidi set her camera on a tripod and filled the viewfinder with

One Wainrich Manor. Everyone found a chair and waited in anticipation. Everyone except Pete—he paced back and forth.

Minutes ticked past in agonizing slowness. Detective Ryan and the twins chatted about the life of a police officer. When your father is the chief of police, talking about policy and procedure becomes second nature.

Midnight came and went. Pete stopped, staring into the darkness, and said, "I think this is a—"

"There he is!" Kathy whispered. The flickering light glowed up through the third-floor dormer window.

"Why are you whispering?" Pete asked. "The thing can't hear you."

"Shut up. And it's not a thing."

Four cellphones lit up with a pixilated rainbow-hued figure moving across the screen. Detective Ryan's eyes locked onto Tom's screen—the thermal-imaging surveillance was a first for him. Heidi hovered over Suzanne, taking in the visual. She grabbed a series of quick shots. The two older ladies sat in silence, enthralled, without saying a word.

"It's a familiar pattern," Suzanne said in a quiet voice. "He starts on the third floor and heads down." Eyes flicked back and forth between the screens and Number One.

"Next stop is the second floor," Tom murmured. The blobby figure formed and morphed, tracing the intruder's path across the third floor. One arm held before it an indistinct shape with a small red-hot dot in the center—the lamp! The figure looked humanlike when it was far from the detector, but became foreshortened and cut off as it closed in. Then the light disappeared from the windows, together with the onscreen image.

"He's on the stairs, heading down to the second floor," Pete said.

The thermal image reappeared on their phones.

"What . . . *wait!*" Tom shouted. "He must've turned around and gone back upstairs. These images are from the third-floor sensor again."

The flickering glow reappeared momentarily in the third-floor dormer window.

"First time we've seen that," Kathy said.

"It's gone again. Now what?" Suzanne asked.

"Heading down, I'd guess," Tom said, sounding perplexed.

"Wandering," Heidi said. *Click.* "Maybe he's looking for something."

"Or someone," Roberta murmured. "Oh, dear." Dorothy glared without saying a word.

"He's back on the second floor," Suzanne said, staring at her screen. "Go figure."

"And there's the light too," Kathy said, pointing. An instant later, the flickering glow and the cellphone thermal images vanished.

"He's heading down into the basement," Pete figured out loud. As before, the intruder appeared to skip the first floor.

"Uh-huh, that's where he is all right," Tom confirmed. "Check your screens." Seconds passed. "He's in the middle of the south wall—he must be right under the coal chute hatch—"

"Now he's backing away," Suzanne said. "He's heading over to the back stairs."

Pete jumped to his feet and raced off, shouting, *"Let's go say hello!"*

16

MAKING AN APPEARANCE

A minute later, Pete yanked hard and cranked left on the hatch. It creaked opened. Tom held it up as Pete all but *dove* into the basement. Kathy headed down the stairs, followed by Suzanne, Heidi, and Detective Ryan. Tom allowed the hatch to close above him and made his way down.

Dorothy unlocked the front door and slipped in behind Roberta.

Soon, multiple beams of light arced around the cavernous space, but there was no saying "hello" to anyone. Once again, the intruder had vanished.

Competing smells reeked downstairs. The Brunellis had noticed the awful stench on their initial visit. "It stinks to high heaven down here," Kathy had complained. But the moldy smell permeating the air was overlaid with a strong odor of kerosene.

"It's the old-fashioned lantern," Pete admitted. "Tom was right."

"That explains the flickering light," Heidi said.

Everyone gathered in a circle on the basement floor. Detective Ryan said, "He's gone—for now, at least. Tom, what did the technology teach us?"

"Quite a bit, actually."

"Really?"

"Yes, sir," Tom replied. "For starters, he's using both sets of stairs, treading back and forth between them."

"What makes you say that?" Pete asked.

Tom pulled out his cellphone and clicked on the thermal surveillance app's icon. He launched the stored streaming footage from the start and held the cell up. "Where does he begin his journey? We see his appearance on the third floor here, in front of the back stairs. But he must have started *elsewhere.*"

"Whoa, I get it!" Suzanne said. "He had to walk *up* to the third floor."

"Exactly," Tom said, "using the back stairs—not the front. I'm willing to bet he's hiding out in the doomsday shelter as we speak. *Why?"*

"Because," Heidi deduced, "he disappeared in the basement."

"Correct."

"Where?" Pete demanded.

In the eerie semidarkness, Tom stepped over to the back flight of stairs. He halted in the space underneath the stairs, beside the first bedroom. "Right here. Behind the stairs it's 'sensor-dark,' because of the placement of the device over there." He pointed to the far corner of the basement, then drew a line with his foot on the floor. "The sensor's grid ends about here. Right where the intruder stepped off our screens—and vanished."

"Well, that makes sense," Dorothy said as she glanced around nervously.

"Let's go to a live view," Tom instructed. All four of the mystery searchers tapped on the app's icon and held their cells up for the others. Pixilated, brightly hued silhouette images appeared, representing all eight members of the team who stood around in the basement, merging weirdly whenever they moved close together. "Check it out as I wave my hand in the air." One of the on-screen figures raised a forelimb. "Now watch as I step into the dark area outside the thermal grid." Tom's thermal avatar vanished.

"Are you saying," Kathy asked softly, "that the intruder is somewhere behind here?" She reached out and touched the stained cement wall with one hand.

Tom hesitated. ". . . Yes, he could well be there. Or very close by."

"Could he be listening to us?" Dorothy asked. "Now? *Right now?*"

"It's possible."

Silence descended upon the group until Roberta spoke up. "What if he climbed over the stair rail and walked back upstairs?"

"Then I don't have an answer," Tom replied, "because he doesn't appear again—anywhere. He seems to have direct access to the doomsday shelter from near the back stairs." For a moment, Tom wished he had focused the thermal sensors to cover the stairwells themselves rather than the open spaces of the mansion, but he kept the thought to himself.

Still, they scoured One Wainrich Manor once more—floor by floor, room by room. The mystery searchers, Detective Ryan, and Heidi combed the basement under the back stairs. And the front ones too—just in case. They tapped on walls and the floor, listening for any sign of a hidden hollow space. But nothing pointed to the existence of a doomsday shelter.

"If there's a shelter down here, it's sure well hidden," Heidi murmured.

Detective Ryan grunted. "Whoever worked on it was a master craftsman."

"It's here," Tom said with confidence. "The permit says so. Count on it."

Something popped into Suzanne's mind. "Who signed that permit?"

"Who cares?" Pete scoffed. "That person's gotta be deader than a doornail.

Kathy poked her brother. "You don't know that."

"I captured an image of the permit . . ." Suzanne said, reaching for her phone. "Here it is: the individual who signed it is E. Ulmer."

"E?" Heidi asked. "An initial, right?

"Right."

Heidi tapped in a Google search on her phone. "There's an E. Ulmer on Fifth Street, just over a mile away."

"If he's our guy, I'll pick him up tomorrow and bring him down here." The detective yawned. "It's been an instructive night, that's for sure. Let's meet back here in the afternoon, right after lunch."

AN HOUR LATER—AFTER THE EXHAUSTED MYSTERY SEARCHERS HAD crashed for the night—the camera app triggered on all four cellphones. Tom sat up in bed, bleary eyed. In the uploaded video, an unknown man came from behind the camera and walked straight to the back door of Number One. Both of his arms grasped a bulging grocery bag.

At the Brunellis' house, Kathy rushed into her brother's bedroom. Pete sat up, his feet on the floor, opening the app. "There's your ghost," he said to his sister. From behind, it appeared the man wore a hat with a wide brim. He had wrapped a scarf around his neck, which hung down over a winter jacket. Estimating height in a video was difficult, but Pete figured he might be a thin six-footer.

"*My ghost?*" Kathy said. "You're the one who called it an 'it.'"

"We can't see his face," Pete grumbled.

The twins absorbed every nuance of the video. "He unlocked nothing," Tom said. The man opened the back door and disappeared into the mansion. "How is that even possible? It was locked when we tried it."

Pete and Kathy called Suzanne's cell. "Did you see it?"

"Uh-huh," Suzanne replied. "He didn't need a key."

"Well," Pete reasoned aloud, "if he was *inside* the mansion, hiding somewhere while we were around, he could have slipped out after we headed out. Which means he left the back door unlocked—on purpose."

"*Hold on,*" Kathy said. "How come the camera only triggered once? He must have left before he came back!"

Tom had the same thought. "Yup. Right after we departed The guy's gotta be keeping tabs on us. He must have unlocked the back door but walked out the *front* door and returned along Pegasus Point Drive."

"Or he could have just slipped out through the coal chute," Pete added.

"*Wait*—he's watching us?" Kathy exclaimed, creeped out. "You can't be *serious!*"

"What's in the grocery bag?" Suzanne asked

"Groceries," Pete replied. "I told you, a guy's gotta eat."

"Well, you sure do," Kathy quipped with a giggle.

"He's buying groceries in the middle of the night?" Suzanne asked.

"Sure," Pete replied. "Think about it. Wainrich Manor is about a mile from that Superstore as you head downtown. And that place is open twenty-four seven."

"That's *great* news," Tom cheered.

"And the reason for that is?"

"Superstores have security cameras. We should get a good look at our intruder tomorrow morning."

17

LEADS TO NOWHERE

On Wednesday morning, the twins dragged themselves out of bed, raced downstairs, and cornered their father at the breakfast table. They poured cereal and popped toast before Tom pulled out his cellphone. He played the video captured hours earlier.

"This is our guy," he said between bites. "He's got his back to us —we still can't see his face. Notice the grocery bag?"

"We think he went grocery shopping at the Superstore," Suzanne explained. "Right after we left the mansion. And if he did, the store security cameras should have video of the guy."

"We need to see those videos, Dad," Tom said.

"I can handle that with a phone call." The Chief paused. "You know what's interesting? He's been—"

"Shadowing us the whole time!" Tom cut in. "He waited until we left, after midnight, before exiting the doomsday shelter to slip out for supplies."

"That's gotta be one heck of a good hiding place," Suzanne said.

"Suzie," Tom suggested, "let's split into teams. You and I'll drive over to the Superstore. Let the Brunellis handle the meeting with Detective Ryan and Mr. Ulmer."

"Deal!"

EDWIN ULMER TURNED OUT TO HAVE REACHED HIS EIGHTY-SEVENTH birthday not long before. "Not bad for an old guy," he said as a way of introduction.

Detective Ryan had just introduced Mr. Ulmer to the Brunellis, Heidi Hoover, Roberta, and Dorothy. The spritely man with sparse white hair and sharp features seemed to have an excellent memory.

"Oh, sure," he said, when he heard Dorothy's name. He focused on her, his eyes twinkling as he spoke. "I remember you as a young 'un. Back then, I worked for your grandfather."

"Nice to meet you again too, Mr. Ulmer," she responded. "I do remember your name. That was a long, long time ago."

"Yes," he replied, "it sure was. No one ever solved the mystery of your grandfather's disappearance, did they?"

"No, sir. Sadly, they did not," she replied.

Mr. Ulmer shook his head. "We all felt the same way. I worked at his company most of my adult life."

"Mr. Ulmer has told me he didn't actually work on the underground shelter," Detective Ryan said, moving the interview along.

"That is correct."

"But you signed the permits," Kathy said.

"Oh, sure," the older man confirmed. "I handled permits on every job at Wainrich Construction."

Heidi asked, "Any idea how long the project ran?"

"Gee, I . . . no, not really, but I'd guess six weeks at a minimum."

"Did you visit the mansion that summer to check on its progress?" Pete asked with a tinge of disappointment in his voice.

THE HAUNTING OF WAINRICH MANOR

"That wasn't part of my job. The superintendent for a project like that would have been Dan Whittier. He passed on years ago. I managed all the administrative work for Wainrich Construction—staffing, ordering materials, permitting, things like that."

"There'd have been other workers, though," Kathy said.

"Yes, ma'am," he replied. "It was a good-size residential project, even for Wainrich Construction."

Detective Ryan wondered, "Would any of them still be around?"

"Doubtful, I'd say."

PRESCOTT'S ONLY SUPERSTORE WAS A QUICK FIFTEEN-MINUTE DRIVE from the Jacksons' house. The twins identified themselves to the store manager. He led them to a security station hidden in a small room next to the optician's clinic.

Inside, two security officers sat in front of a series of large flat-screen monitors. One of them stood and introduced himself. "Hi, I'm Ray Wintering. I understand you're looking for one of our customers. How can I help?"

Tom and Suzanne shook hands with Ray and brought him up to date. "We think the suspect shopped for groceries around one o'clock this morning."

"Well, if he did, he won't be hard to find," Ray said. "There're not a lot of grocery shoppers at that hour. A few, but . . . here, pull up chairs in front of this monitor."

The touchscreen monitor displayed a grid of twenty different video feeds. Tom, always enthralled with technology, had a question. "Does each live feed come from a different camera?"

"Uh-huh. We've got a camera on every corridor and each register," Mr. Wintering replied. "Plus the self-checkout area, both entrances and exits, and the parking lot." He glanced over at them.

"If your guy showed, we've got him covered. You said one a.m., right?"

"Yes, sir," Suzanne replied.

"Here we go. Let's expand the footage showing the two entrances, starting five minutes earlier." He tap-tapped the screen and keyed in the time code.

Seconds ticked by on an embedded digital clock. The three sat in silence. Two individuals and a young couple wandered in before the time clock registered 1:00 a.m. "Not him?" Ray asked.

"Nope."

Another three minutes passed before the twins leaned closer. "That's our guy," Tom murmured.

"It sure is," Suzanne said. "But look at those sunglasses."

A tall, obviously elderly man, very thin, ambled through the south entranceway, unaware of the hidden camera aimed straight toward him. *Or was he?* He wore his fedora-style hat with the brim pulled low, and a scarf wrapped around his neck that extended up to his chin. And sunglasses. *Huge.*

The man grabbed a grocery cart and turned right. "Geez," Tom complained. "There's no way we'll be able to identify this guy."

"He's gotta be in his seventies, at least," Ray said. "He doesn't look like a criminal. What'd he do?"

"He moved into an abandoned mansion, uninvited," said Tom.

Suzanne had a question. "Would a late-night shopper wearing sunglasses trigger security's suspicion?"

"Nope. You'd be amazed at what we see here. Some people are just eccentric, others have legit vision problems that make them wear shades. He's heading to the groceries." Ray touched the screen to expand a video image from the fruits and vegetables section. The unknown man walked toward the camera, his entire body captured at a forty-five-degree angle. For the next ten minutes, he trailed up and down corridors, selecting a handful of items and dropping them into his cart. In the cereal aisle, they watched him pick up three boxes of corn flakes. In the dairy aisle, he grabbed two gallons of milk.

"That won't last long," Tom said. "I'll bet anything he shows up a couple times a week."

Minutes later, the man self-checked his groceries, taking his time packing them into a single bag. He pushed a couple of bills into the kiosk's payment device and collected his change. Then he nudged the empty cart aside, turned his back, and exited the store.

"Where's he going now?" Suzanne asked, leaning closer to the screen.

Ray enlarged the image from an exterior feed to capture the subject as he turned left and walked along the Superstore's front sidewalk. The man headed into the parking lot and disappeared down an adjoining side street.

"On his way back to Wainrich Manor," Tom said.

AFTER RUNNING MR. ULMER HOME, DETECTIVE RYAN RETURNED TO Wainrich Manor, arriving just before the twins. The group caught up with one another. The frustration level had cranked higher.

"Well," Tom said, "we're kinda stuck, aren't we? Mr. Ulmer doesn't know where the doomsday shelter is. And there's no way to identify the intruder from the Superstore's security cameras."

"So what now?" Suzanne asked.

"Now we go in there and corner him," Pete said. "Wrestle the guy down to the ground. I think that's obvious."

His sister tossed her head. "It might be obvious to you, but I have no intention of going back at midnight and wrestling anyone."

Pete coughed. "Tom and I'll do it."

"No you won't," Suzanne corrected him. "Not without me."

"Why not throw a party and invite everyone?" Kathy quipped.

"Count me in," Dorothy said, raising her hand.

That sent Heidi into a fit of spontaneous laughter. Her tight, black curls bounced around her head. "I'm coming too."

"The more, the merrier," Pete said. "If we don't flush him out, we'll never solve this mystery."

All eyes landed on Detective Ryan. "What say you?" Suzanne asked.

The detective hesitated. Somewhere in Roberta's house, a mantel clock ticked loudly. "Well, we won't tackle anyone, but I agree with Pete. Whoever this individual is, we've got a lost soul." He paused for a bit. "So yeah, I think we should come up with a plan to confront him."

18

PANDEMONIUM!

That night, the plan unfolded as expected—*until it didn't*. The adventure began with the entire surveillance team gathering in front of Number One at 11:40 p.m.

"The last thing we want is to scare this guy," Tom said, his voice low. "It's important that he doesn't realize we're in there and covering every floor."

"Before we head in," Heidi said, "I'd still like to know something. Is the intruder friend or foe."

"Neither," Suzanne replied. "If he were friendly, he would have identified himself by now. And if he were dangerous—"

"Bunker would have paid a price," Pete said. "But he didn't."

"Maybe he's just a freeloader," Dorothy whispered harshly. "Some guy who moved in because he saw an opportunity!"

Ryan shook his head. "We don't know. But we have to be ready for anything."

Dorothy unlocked the mansion's front doors before opening one wide enough for the group to slip through in single file. The Chief and Ryan led the way into the cold, dead-quiet house without a word crossing anyone's lips.

Even the grandfather clock in the hallway—with its jarring *bong, bong, bong* that resonated throughout the mansion—had wound down. *No tick-tock.*

The group split up as everyone headed toward his or her pre-assigned location. The boys made their way to the back stairs and crept halfway down into the basement, settling down with their backs against the cold concrete wall. With no windows—nothing but the grimy glass hatch providing a glimmer of muted moonlight —they found themselves shrouded in almost total darkness.

The cellar continued to stink to high heaven. *What is that smell, anyway?* Pete wondered. They hadn't given it much thought.

Tom got comfortable before he touched the infrared app's icon on his phone's screen, with the brightness preset just above minimum. The thermal sensor on the basement level showed nothing, of course. He could see the slightly pixilated images of the other members of the team in place on the main, second, and third floors. Everything, he realized, was as it should be. The boys sat back and waited. Even Pete remained still, trying not to move a muscle.

Meanwhile, the girls headed over to the *front* stairs, accompanied by Heidi Hoover, camera in hand. The three made their way halfway down into the basement and chose spots on the wooden steps. They settled down without a peep—Suzanne closer to the basement floor, Heidi two steps up, and Kathy higher still. *The basement's silent as a grave,* Kathy thought with a slight shudder.

Suzanne zipped up her down jacket and folded her arms. *It's freezing down here.*

Detective Ryan and the Chief posted themselves on the main floor. Ryan guarded the back stairs, while the Chief watched the front. Each stood ready to race up or down at a moment's notice— if, or when, the intruder appeared.

Roberta hunkered down on the second floor between the two sets of stairs. She had dragged a dusty armchair from the master bedroom, trying her best not to make a sound, and placed it in the hallway equidistant between the stairs. Then she brushed away the dust before sinking into the cushions, pulling a blanket over her for warmth. "If I have to stay up past midnight looking for an intruder," she had told Dorothy as the team chose their surveillance locations earlier that evening, "I'm going to make sure I'm comfortable."

Meanwhile, Dorothy had positioned herself on the third floor, hiding behind a bedroom door just a few feet away from the central dormer window. She stood like a sentinel, holding a slender, eighteen-inch-tall glass vase she had found in her old bedroom. Both hands grasped the vase in a firm grip. "If the intruder comes near me, he'll regret it," she had told Roberta. She meant it too. "I'll be ready for him."

Time crawled as they waited in the darkness. Midnight came and went. Pete counted the minutes to himself as they ticked past. *Twelve-oh-one . . . twelve-oh-two . . . twelve-oh-three . . .* Then—in the basement—Heidi and the mystery searchers heard a strange clicking sound . . . something they had never heard before. Kathy frowned and braced herself. Seconds passed, but nothing happened.

Dorothy screamed! Pandemonium broke loose inside One Wainrich Manor.

The two police officers jumped onto the stairs and raced up, the boys right behind them. Kathy followed with Heidi at her heels. Heidi touched the video icon on her camera and began recording as she ran. Roberta stood, too frightened to move, as everyone rushed past.

Suzanne froze. The clicking sound. *What was it?* And there was something else too. An unusual smell . . . toothpaste? She turned just as someone bumped into her from behind. Too shocked even to scream, she flailed—desperately trying not to lose her balance— before tumbling backward.

Everything went dark.

SUZANNE OPENED HER EYES. THE STRONG ODOR OF KEROSENE FUEL filled her nostrils as a flickering light projected the shadow of a man's head and shoulders against a wall. She was, she realized, lying flat on her back, close to the ground. On a mattress. A lantern rested on the concrete floor, illuminating a small room, its door open to the basement. Everything swirled around in a crazy, dizzying circle. She tried to focus on the face above her. Warm, worried eyes looked down at her.

"I—I—I'm sorry," he said.

Suzanne reached up to discover a cold, wet washcloth on her forehead. His face looked vaguely familiar. "What did you do?" she wondered out loud.

"I—I— b-bumped into you. Didn't know . . . you were there. You—you fell b-b-backward."

Oh sure, she thought. In her mind, the jigsaw pieces began falling into place. *The strange clicking sound. The stairs. A woman screaming. Someone behind her.*

"That's not your fault." Suzanne tried sitting up, but dizziness engulfed her, pushing her back down. Her head throbbed. She closed her eyes for what seemed like mere seconds. When she opened them again, the tiny room had inexplicably filled up with familiar faces, all staring down at her with concern. Three of them materialized beside her.

Kathy held on to her hand. "Are you okay, Suzanne?"

"What happened?" her father demanded gruffly.

"Are you hurt?" her worried brother asked.

"I'm . . . fine." She winced. *He* was still there. Her eyes flicked over to the man's face. For the first time, she noticed tears rolling over his high, prominent cheekbones. "I fell down the stairs. This man picked me up and carried me in here." She reached up and once more felt the cold, damp washcloth. "He placed this on my forehead."

The Chief thrust his hand out to the stranger. "Thank you, sir." The man took his hand and murmured, "My—my fault."

With a struggle, Suzanne pushed herself up onto one elbow. "No, it wasn't. You bumped into me in the dark without knowing I was there. You're Bill Wainrich, aren't you?"

19

REVELATIONS

Suzanne spent the next few hours at Prescott Regional Hospital. She hadn't broken any bones in her fall, but she had a mild concussion—and a headache that refused to go away until the following day.

"Good thing," Suzanne said. The girls were on their way to Wainrich Manor. "I *so* wanted to get together with everyone. It's quite a celebration, isn't it?"

"It sure—oh, my gosh," Kathy exclaimed as she cranked the Mustang into the cul-de-sac. "Look at all the cars! There's your Chevy—the boys are already here."

The Chief's recent birthday party—the event that had triggered the investigation into the "haunting" of Wainrich Manor—seemed like a distant memory. "And yet it was only a week ago," Suzanne said. "So much has happened since then, and now we're celebrating again. *Can you believe it?*"

The same group had gathered once more, but the number of revelers had grown by four. Detective Ryan had arrived much earlier. Heidi ducked through the front door as the girls came to a stop. And, of course, the list included Dorothy and her brother,

Bill, the reunited siblings who hadn't seen each other in more than half a century.

Kathy blinked. "Well, look at that. Lights are on inside the mansion."

"That means they should have the heat on."

"I almost froze to death in there more than once," Kathy said with a laugh.

"Roberta told me they've been cleaning since early this morning."

Kathy parked on the cul-de-sac, right behind a van marked Pest Control. "You know what that means," Suzanne said with a wry smile.

The girls walked to the front door. A posted sign read, Please Come In. They stepped into the spacious hallway and ran smack into Roberta, who greeted them with big hugs. "Isn't it grand!" she said, her enthusiasm brimming over. "It's like the old days!"

The girls glanced at each other in astonishment. Half a dozen children raced up and down the stairs. "Brenda's kids," Roberta explained, seeing their facial expressions. "The family returned to Number Two. Come into the kitchen and I'll introduce you."

The house felt warm as toast, forcing the girls to peel off their jackets. In the mansion's supersize kitchen, they found the Chief, Joe Brunelli, and Detective Ryan, sitting at the table with hands wrapped around coffee cups and munching fresh-baked banana bread. Sherri and Maria chatted with a middle-aged woman. Overhead, fluorescent lights brightened the old-fashioned kitchen, bathing the archaic appliances in bright white.

"Excuse me, Brenda," Roberta said. "Please meet Suzanne and Kathy, the other half of the mystery searchers team."

"Oh, hello," Brenda said with a warm smile. She stood and held out her hand. "I met your brothers, and they told me all about you." She looked closely at Suzanne. "I understand the hospital gave you a clean bill of health. Thank goodness!"

"Yes, thank you. Everything's fine."

Dorothy rushed in and cornered the girls. "Someone wants to see you. Follow me." The kitchen emptied as everyone followed Dorothy down the wide hallway—past the grandfather clock *tick-tock-ing* away—and into the living room.

Bill sat next to Heidi Hoover on the sofa. The boys had pulled up a couple of chairs in front of them. "Hey!" Pete called out to the girls. "Bill's filling in a few blanks in his history."

"And it's pretty interesting," Tom added.

Suzanne and Kathy shook hands with Bill. He smiled when he spotted Suzanne. "You—you're okay?"

"Yes, I am, Bill. I'm fine, thanks to you. And thank you for asking."

The Chief and Detective Joe Ryan had debriefed Bill earlier that morning. They stood next to the siblings' father, Joe, close to the fireplace. Everyone else surged forward and found seats.

"What did you learn?" Maria asked.

Pete explained. "Well, Bill told us he went AWOL from the Navy in Greece."

"Y—yes, I did," he replied. "B-b-big mistake."

"Then what happened?"

He looked away for a few seconds, seemingly trying to form words in his mind. Dorothy sat down and slipped one arm around her brother's shoulders.

"I . . . f-found work on ships . . . and . . . in the d-dockyard. I drove a truck from Turkey . . . heading into Greece. Turkish p-p-police arrested me . . . for carrying contraband. But . . . I didn't know what I was doing. I needed . . . w-work. Very s-s-serious charge in Turkey. They gave me . . . life. Fifty years. Wanted to use me . . . as an example."

"Fifty years!" Maria exclaimed in horror.

Heidi scanned the appalled faces. "This guy really paid the price."

The Chief added, "He served time in an infamous Istanbul prison, known as one of the worst in the world."

Over the next hour, Bill explained, as best as he could, about his life sentence behind bars—for a crime he hadn't committed. He skipped through the years that had stretched into decades. "I try not to . . . think about all that t-time. It's not—not worth remembering," he declared. Then the magic day came for his release—a month earlier.

"They returned my expired p-passport, so I could get the American embassy in Istanbul to issue me a new one . . . and my m-money, old bills I had to exchange at a bank for new ones. I . . . bought clothes . . . and a t-t-ticket to L.A. On a freighter. Then I hitchhiked to Prescott. Thought"—he turned toward his sister —"Dorothy might live . . . here. That I could make amends. When I realized . . . it was deserted, I m-moved in."

Suzanne asked, "In all those years, you never tried to connect with Dorothy?"

He looked down before answering. "I left . . . on terrible terms. Came back . . . for forgiveness. But once I was here, I realized . . . I d-didn't know how to find her."

Dorothy hugged her brother as tears rolled down her cheeks.

"What about the U.S. State Department?" Joe asked. "Couldn't they help?"

"They . . . tried," Bill answered. "Often . . . but the government over there . . . refused to c-c-cooperate. Eventually, the embassy gave up on me."

"How did you get in here?" Maria asked.

"The coal chute."

Pete nodded to himself. *Yup.*

"You often wandered around the mansion late at night," Sherri said. "With a lantern. W*hy?*"

"Freezing in here," Bill replied. "Movement . . . kept me warm. And . . . it was hard for me to sleep."

"Why did you wind up the grandfather clock?" Kathy asked. "It's so spooky!"

"M-made me feel . . . less alone," Bill said.

"We spotted you opening and closing the hatch one night," Kathy said. "But we didn't see *you*."

"Awful smell . . ." he replied. "Tried to . . . air it out, but that hatch is heavy. Pushed it up with . . . a stick."

Pete and Kathy glanced at each other with knowing looks. *Okay. Wow.*

Suzanne had a question. "You slept upstairs, but you moved to the doomsday shelter. We wondered why."

Bill looked at his sister, trying to understand. "The underground shelter," she explained.

"Oh, sure. Kept hearing p-people . . . every day or two . . . coming into the house. Or walking around. A man . . . scared me. So I hid out downstairs. I left him . . . a message."

"You wrote 'Get out' in the dust on the dining room table," said Heidi.

"Yes."

"And you spoke those words aloud too," Suzanne added, "from a hiding place—"

"Yes, just outside the d-d-dining room," Bill said.

"Is that why you never walked around at night on the ground floor?" Suzanne asked. "Because you were afraid of running into the man who scared you?"

"Yes," Bill said with a dead serious expression.

Tom asked, "How did you know about the shelter?"

"Grandpa showed me . . . at the end of summer. Before the accident. He . . . said it was a s-s-secret, told me not to tell anyone . . . yet. So I didn't."

The Chief spoke up. "Bill, any idea what happened to your grandfather?"

"N—no," Bill replied. "Dor— Dorothy and I talked about it . . . but . . . no clue."

"And there never will be," his sister added firmly. "We've agreed to let it go. It's too far in the past."

Detective Ryan asked, "There's one thing I forgot to ask you, Bill. The night before last, you opened the shelter's door. People heard that clicking sound. Then Dorothy screamed—"

"You'd holler too if a rat ran up your leg," Dorothy cut in, causing everyone to burst into laughter.

The detective smiled. "Anyway, instead of ducking back into the shelter, you closed its door and then headed up the stairs. That's when you bumped into Suzanne."

"Yes . . . I did."

"Why didn't you return to the shelter?"

He turned once more to his sister. "I had to find out . . . *who* had screamed. The day before I thought I heard Dorothy's voice . . . thought she had r-r-returned." He smiled again. "She had."

The time slipped by. The Chief rushed away after a call from headquarters. Minutes later, the pest control man headed out. "I've set traps everywhere, ma'am. I'll be back tomorrow."

Dorothy informed everyone that she would be moving back into One Wainrich Manor. "I'll look after Bill until his health returns. We'll fix the place up—together."

Roberta cheered. "Families I've known most of my life will occupy the three homes on the manor. For the first time in sixty years! Isn't it wonderful?"

Bill offered to show anyone interested how the hidden entrance to the doomsday shelter worked. The entire group followed him into the basement. Fluorescent fixtures overhead lit up the cavernous area. Bill ducked under the back stairs and stopped beside the stained concrete wall.

"Tom," Pete said, "looks like you were right on the money."

Bill reached over to touch the wall in the corner under the

stairs. He pushed on it with a closed fist at eye level. With a grinding sound, a six-inch square block of concrete slid inward, barely an inch. Then, seconds later, an entire section of the wall— five feet wide, floor to ceiling—glided back about three inches and slid to one side, *with a clicking sound,* into a socket inside the wall.

"Ingenious!" Tom said. "No wonder we couldn't find it."

"Holy doodle," said Heidi. She held her camera up high. *Click. Click.*

Pete, ever the aspiring engineer, exclaimed, *"Whoa!* A secret sliding pocket door in the wall! Why didn't I think of that?"

"Wait!" Suzanne said. "This place had no electricity for decades. Don't you need power to operate the door?"

"It's a *doomsday* shelter," Pete replied. "I bet Mr. Wainrich antici-pated an emergency without power. Someone in his company engineered a concealed block-and-tackle system for him, using weights and pulleys inside the wall, entirely mechanical."

"Amazing," Kathy exclaimed.

Suzanne wrinkled her nose. "That awful smell. *What is it?"*

"Standing water," Pete replied.

"I don't see any," Suzanne said.

"You wouldn't, not in winter," he said. "Notice how you step *down* into the shelter? Its floor is a foot lower than the basement floor. In spring and summer, if there's any water seepage, it would collect here and cause mildew. The stench remains even when the water's gone—it gets in the walls. Probably attracted the rats too. No wonder it stinks down here. Just as I figured all along."

"Excuse me," Kathy said, giving him some serious side-eye. *"You* figured? All along?"

EXCERPT FROM BOOK 11

THE DAYLIGHT HEIST ON WHISKEY ROW

CHAPTER 1

Saturday, July 4

"*Nice.* I like it!" Pete Brunelli exclaimed as he circled float number thirty-three. "Are we good, or what?" Minutes earlier, the mystery searchers had reached the staging area for Prescott's annual Frontier Days Parade. The next challenge was to find their entry among two hundred others. Turned out that thirty-three wasn't far from the front. *There.* They breathed an enormous sigh of relief. Had they missed the start time, well...

"Whoa, check it out," Suzanne Jackson said, gazing up at the huge float, decorated with hundreds of multi-colored flowers. Hanging above it was a gigantic helium balloon that rocked in a gentle summer breeze. Twin messages on the back and front read: *The Daily Pilot, Your Hometown Newspaper.* Complimentary graphics ran along the base of the float, celebrating the newspaper's theme, "good news." Headlines from the past read, *Prescott wins national award, State championship coming to our city,* and *A great place to live.*

A small Central Arizona city nestled in a mile-high basin among pine-dotted mountains, Prescott is home to "the world's oldest rodeo"—cowboy country, for sure. And today, celebrating that heritage, the summer parade was scheduled to kick off at 9:00 a.m. sharp. The procession would lead off with a color guard of veterans, followed by the mayor and members of city council. Equestrian units, marching bands, dance troupes, and drill teams —and a phalanx of clowns—would all be interspersed at intervals.

Float thirty-three had appeared in every Frontier Days parade since anyone could remember. This time, instead of watching from the sidelines, the foursome would ride on it. *A first.*

Pete's sister, Kathy, agreed with her best friend. "Oh—my— gosh. It's even better in bright sunlight. We could even take first place!"

Tom, Suzanne's twin brother—he was the thoughtful, quiet one of the four—chuckled. "It couldn't be because we did most of the work on it, could it?" The mystery searchers had spent days getting the truck-drawn float ready.

In a single bound, Pete jumped up onto the float's platform. "Hey, give credit where credit's due, I always say. At least we didn't have to create the thing from scratch." True enough; the news- paper recycled the same float year after year, always with a fresh new theme. Pete held one hand out to his sister and yanked her up. "Hey, what happened to Heidi?"

"No clue. We might have to start without her."

Ever since starting at Prescott High, the Jackson and Brunelli foursome had teamed up to solve mysteries and fight crime. *The Daily Pilot,* Prescott's hometown newspaper, and its star reporter, Heidi Hoover, had covered their cases, plastering them across the front page. It was Heidi—who had soon become a best friend and often a fellow investigator—who had dubbed them "the mystery searchers." The name had stuck.

Heidi had called three weeks earlier with an invitation to ride in the parade—on the newspaper's float. "I think you'd all love it—it's a riot. The crowds are huge and it's pretty much a fun time." The foursome had jumped at the opportunity.

"We've never done anything like that before," a delighted Suzanne said.

"For sure," Kathy said with a giggle. "Although we've *attended* every Frontier Days parade since the beginning of time."

Tom nodded, glancing over to his sister. "Same here, right Suzie? I don't think we've ever missed one."

"Just our vacation in eighth grade," she reminded.

"There's, uh, just one thing," Heidi added, lowering her voice as if sharing a secret. "We could use a little help putting the float together."

Much later, after their third day of redecorating, Pete moaned, "Oh, *I* get it. This is a carrot—and—stick deal. We get to ride in the parade, but first she'll work us to death." Still, it turned out to be a lot of fun, and well worth the effort.

On the morning of the parade, the foursome set out for the staging area in two cars. Suzanne drove the twins' Chevy with every intention of arriving early but finding a parking place proved next to impossible. The downtown parade route traveled along Willis, Marina, Gurley, and Montezuma Streets, all of which were closed to vehicular traffic.

"*Sheesh,*" Suzanne groused before heading away from the area. "We're gonna have to park a mile away. We can't afford to be late. The parade starts at nine o'clock."

"Go north," Tom advised. They drove another four blocks before nosing the Chevy into a tight parking place on a side street. Pete found a spot a half block further and parked the Mustang.

The foursome hiked back, passing throngs of people hugging

the city sidewalks. Countless lawn chairs lined the route, music blared, and kids screamed as they raced around. The anticipation level ran high.

Hot dog and hamburger grills had sprung up in a carnival atmosphere, and delicious smells wafted through the streets.

"Way too early," Kathy complained, wrinkling her nose.

Pete had already stopped to grab a hot dog. "Are you serious? It's *never* too early for a dog. *This is breakfast!*" He slathered the bun with onions, relish, and mustard before licking his fingers noisily. His sister rolled her eyes.

They arrived, at last. Late. The kind of late that's not fun. Still, at least they made it.

"Two minutes after the start time," Suzanne said, glancing at her cellphone. "Way too close for comfort. I wonder what happened to—"

"Heidi!" Pete shouted. "Come on up."

The diminutive star reporter raced over, her tight black curls bouncing around her head. "Sorry! We couldn't find anywhere to park."

"Tell us about it," Tom said. "There's a ton of people out here."

Heidi introduced the man who arrived with her. "This is Fred Myer, one of our press operators. He'll be driving the truck today."

"Hi, Fred!" the foursome chorused.

"Hi, y'all," he shouted with a wave. "You ready to roll?"

"You're just in time," Kathy said. "The line's starting to move."

"Okay," Fred said. He jumped into the truck's cabin and fired up the engine.

Heidi held out a hand and Tom pulled her up top. Seconds later, they were on their way. *"Whoo-hoo."*

Float thirty-three found itself sandwiched between Prescott High's marching band and the equestrian unit of Yavapai County's search and rescue squad. Cries of "Hello!" and "Have fun!" rang out from the band members. "I swear we know every one of 'em," Kathy said with a smile.

The clip-clop of horses' hooves on pavement clashed with the band warming up—a cacophony of snare drums, the deep tone of the bass drum, clanging cymbals, insistent trumpets, trombones, clarinets, and flutes. Then, as the parade turned onto Willis Street —right where the major crowds formed—everything changed. The band broke into the "Colonel Bogie March," a raucous chorus with trumpets and drums that drowned out the sound of the horses.

"And everything else," Pete said good-naturedly.

The five stood on the float's platform, waving to the crowds as the float glided past. A few kids from the Jackson neighborhood ran alongside the float until Fred shooed them away. Every so often, one person or another called out, "Hi, Pete!" or "Hey, Suzanne!" Quite a few people knew one or the other of the four-some, and Heidi had lots of newspaper fans. In just a few years she had emerged as a well-known Prescott personality.

At two-point-five miles per hour, the parade leisurely wound down Willis, Carlton, and Cortez Streets before turning onto Montezuma Street—home to Prescott's famous Whiskey Row. The street had earned its moniker after a fire burned down the entire block in 1900 before quickly being resurrected with some forty new saloons. Today, it's a shopping mecca and one of Arizona's favorite tourist destinations.

The crowds grew larger, and the noise increased. The band had graduated to "The Stars and Stripes Forever." Trumpets blared and big bass drums resonated with patriotic gusto, and the snare drums beat out their staccato flourishes. As they rolled past the county courthouse on their left, Suzanne noticed that the hands on the courthouse's giant clock pointed to 9:37 a.m.

Then, from somewhere, a new sound occurred—a strange *boom.* "What's that?" Kathy asked, puzzled.

"Who cares?" Pete replied flippantly, waving to the crowds.

Suzanne yelled over to her brother. "You pick up on anything?"

Tom focused on the street ahead. "Check out the crowd, farther up, to your right." There, heads had swiveled away to glimpse something behind them.

The parade ground to an unexpected halt. The marching band stopped, and the chorus petered out with a few more drumbeats. Trumpets halted in mid-phrase. Fred braked. Behind thirty-three, horses whinnied and stomped their hooves. The crowd had grown quieter and restless. People looked around in confusion.

An alarm, loud and insistent, rang out along Whiskey Row.

Heidi leaped off the float and onto the pavement, yelling, "*C'mon!* Something's happening!" The mystery searchers vaulted to the ground and tore after the star reporter.

Pete shouted, *"Where?"*

"Past the restaurant, on the right!"

Heidi reached Birksen Jewelers and pushed through a mob that had gathered at the front door. The foursome squeezed in behind. Inside the store, an ear-piercing alarm shrieked, all but drowning out the ringing of multiple phones. People yelled to make themselves heard. *Total bedlam,* Suzanne thought.

A man wearing a white shirt lay face down on the floor, eyes closed. Blood streamed from a nasty gash on the crown of his head. Two women—clerks, by the way they dressed, Kathy figured—were applying paper towels to the man's wound.

Suzanne's eyes shot over to Pete. "Get the search and rescue crew!" she shouted. "They're right behind our float!" Pete pushed his way back out the front door.

The girls knelt to help stem the bleeding. One clerk got to her feet and hurried toward the rear of the store. She used a key to access a small metal panel and killed the alarm. Seconds earlier, the ringing phones had died away. A strange, surreal silence descended upon the store's interior.

A miniature camera appeared as if by magic in Heidi's hand. *Click. Click.*

Tom took in the shocking scene before him. He counted eleven display cases smashed wide open—ransacked and empty—but three others, loaded with glittering merchandise, untouched. *Strange.* A million tiny pieces of glass carpeted the floor, crunching under the soles of his shoes. He spotted multiple cameras, all positioned closer to the ceiling. And then there was the—

"Look!" Heidi exclaimed. *Click.* "Someone blew the back door open." A thin layer of soot covered the rear security door, agape about a foot to the outside. In his mind, Tom replayed the boom sound. *Oh, okay,* he thought. *Got it.*

The clerk who had killed the alarm was a short middle-aged woman, dressed in low-heeled shoes, a skirt, and a matching blouse and wearing bright red lipstick that contrasted starkly with her pasty, white skin and pixie-cut dark hair. Drops of blood had found their way onto her powder-blue blouse. She seemed disoriented.

Tom caught her eye. "Did you see what happened?" he asked quietly. He noticed her nametag: Carol Williams, Birksen Jewelers.

"No," she replied in a shaky voice. "Donna and I were standing in the doorway, watching the parade. Mr. Evers—he's the one on the floor, our manager—was on the sidewalk when a cannon went off. I thought it was like, you know, part of the clown act. Then I heard something else. I glanced back into the store and . . . it—it was just horrid! Two masked men wearing dark clothing were smashing the display cases open with sledgehammers. So frightening." She stopped and took a deep breath.

"What happened next?" Tom urged.

"I screamed!"

I hope you have enjoyed this sneak peek at book 11 in
The Mystery Searchers Family Book Series

The Daylight Heist on Whiskey Row

To be released summer 2022

BIOGRAPHY

Barry Forbes began his writing career in 1980, eventually scripting and producing hundreds of film and video corporate presentations, winning a handful of industry awards along the way. At the same time, he served as an editorial writer for Tribune Newspapers and wrote his first two books, both non-fiction.

In 1997, he founded and served as CEO for Sales Simplicity Software, a market leader which was sold two decades later.

What next? "I always loved mystery stories and one of my favorite places to visit was Prescott, Arizona. It's situated in rugged central Arizona with tremendous locales for mysteries." In 2017, Barry merged his interest in mystery and his skills in writing, adding in a large dollop of technology. The Mystery Searchers Family Book Series was born.

Barry's wife, Linda, passed in 2019 and the series is dedicated to her. "Linda proofed the initial drafts of each book and acted as my chief advisor." The couple had been married for 49 years and had two children. A number of their fifteen grandchildren provided feedback on each book.

Contact Barry: barry@mysterysearchers.com

ALSO BY BARRY FORBES

The Mystery Searchers Family Book Series

BOOK 1: THE MYSTERY ON APACHE CANYON DRIVE

A small child wanders out onto a busy Arizona highway! In a hair-raising rescue, sixteen-year-old twins Tom and Suzanne Jackson save the little girl from almost certain death. Soon, the brother-and-sister team up with their best friends, Kathy and Pete Brunelli, on a perilous search for the child's mother—and her past. The mystery deepens as one case becomes two, forcing the four friends to deploy concealed technological tools along Apache Canyon Drive. The danger level ramps up with the action, and the "mystery searchers" are born.

BOOK 2: THE GHOST IN THE COUNTY COURTHOUSE

A mysterious "ghost" bypasses the security system of the Yavapai Courthouse Museum and makes off with four of the museum's most precious Native American relics. At the invitation of the museum's curator, Dr. William Wasson, the mystery searchers jump onto the case and deploy a range of technological devices to discover the ghost's secrets. If the ghost strikes again, the museum's very future is in doubt. A dangerous game of cat and mouse ensues.

BOOK 3: THE SECRETS OF THE MYSTERIOUS MANSION

Heidi Hoover, a good friend and a top reporter for Prescott's newspaper, *The Daily Pilot*, introduces the mystery searchers to a mysterious mansion in the forest—at midnight! The mansion is under siege from unknown "hunters." *Who are they? What are they searching for?* Good old-fashioned detective work and a couple of technological tricks ultimately reveal the truth. A desperate race ensues, but time is running out . . .

BOOK 4: THE HOUSE ON CEMETERY HILL

There's a dead man walking, and it's up to the mystery searchers to figure out why. That's the challenge set by Mrs. Leslie McPherson, a successful but eccentric Prescott businesswoman. The mystery searchers team up with their favorite detective and use technology to spy on high-tech criminals at Cemetery Hill. It's a perilous game with heart-stopping moments of danger.

BOOK 5: THE TREASURE OF SKULL VALLEY

Suzanne discovers a map hidden in the pages of a classic old book at the thrift store where she works. It's titled "My Treasure Map" and leads past Skull Valley, twenty miles west of Prescott, and into the high-desert country—to an unexpected, shocking, and elusive treasure. "Please help," the note begs. The mystery searchers utilize the power and reach of the internet to trace the movement of people and events . . . half a century earlier.

BOOK 6: THE VANISHING IN DECEPTION GAP

A text message to Kathy sets off a race into the unknown. "There are pirates operating out here and they're dangerous. I can't prove it but I need your help." Who sent the message? Out where? Pirates—on land! How weird is that? The mystery searchers dive in, but it might be too late. Whoever sent the message has vanished into thin air.

BOOK 7: THE GETAWAY LOST IN TIME

A stray dog saves the twins from a dangerous predator on the hiking trail at Watson Lake. In a surprising twist, the dog leads the mystery searchers to the recent suspicious death of an elderly recluse with a mysterious past. The four young sleuths join the Sheriff's Office of Yavapai County and Heidi Hoover, the star reporter of *The Daily Pilot*, in the search for the heartless perpetrator who caused her death.

BOOK 8: THE HUNT FOR THE ELUSIVE MASTERMIND

The mystery searchers embark on one of their strangest cases—the kidnapping of the wife of one of the city's most prominent bankers. The mystery deepens as the baffling questions emerge: Who are the kidnappers—beneath their disguises? What happened to the ransom money? It soon becomes clear that the hostage may not be the only one in danger . . .

BOOK 9: THE LEGEND OF RATTLER MINE

In a rocky ravine north of the Flying W Dude Ranch, the mystery searchers save an unconscious man from certain death. Little do they know that they're about to step into a century-old legend that's far more dangerous than it first appears. Does Rattler Mine really exist? If it does, exactly where is it? And who is the mysterious man—or woman—willing to risk everything for it . . . *no matter the cost?*

BOOK 10: THE HAUNTING OF WAINRICH MANOR

It's the Chief's birthday party, and the Jackson and Brunelli families gather to celebrate at his favorite restaurant. Little do they know that they are about to cross paths with the charming Mrs. Roberta Robertson, who will introduce the mystery searchers to a bizarre case. Someone is haunting One Wainrich Manor, a mansion abandoned for sixty years. *Who and why?*

BOOK 11: THE DAYLIGHT HEIST ON WHISKEY ROW (COMING SUMMER, 2022)

A daring daylight heist takes place along Prescott's Whiskey Row during the annual Frontier Days parade. Detective Joe Ryan believes the million-dollar robbery is a professional hit, executed by out-of-town criminals. *But is it?* The mystery searchers take on one of their most puzzling cases yet.

DON'T FORGET...

Don't forget to check out
www.MysterySearchers.com

Register to receive updates on The Mystery Searchers Family Book Series. You'll also find a wealth of information on the website, including stills and video scenes of Prescott, reviews, press releases, rewards, and more.

Questions or comments? My email address: barry@mysterysearchers.com

Are you enjoying this series? Please do me a huge favor and do a quick review. They really make a difference!